THE LEGACY SERIES

Series Titles

The Plagues
Joe Baumann

Sometimes Creek
Steve Fox

Finding the Bones
Nikki Kallio

The Clayfields
Elise Gregory

Kind of Blue
Christopher Chambers

Evangelina Everyday
Dawn Burns

Township
Jamie Lyn Smith

Responsible Adults
Patricia Ann McNair

Great Escapes from Detroit
Joseph O'Malley

Nothing to Lose
Kim Suhr

The Appointed Hour
Susanne Davis

Praise for
The Plagues

Strange and terrible things happen to ordinary people, and they deal. Rivers of blood, flies, frogs, hail, darkness at noon and yes, locusts – plagues that descend on all, but are experienced individually, as plagues are. There's a superficial whimsy, a strange mixture of chaos and control, but also a deep seriousness. Over and again, Baumann's characters reach across the ever-widening gulfs opened by the ever-increasing weirdness of their worlds for human connection, sometimes successfully, sometimes not, but that's where the hope lies.

—Adam Brooke Davis
editor of *Green Hills Literary Lantern*

Joe Baumann's short story collection is a fantastic, modern take on the Plagues of Egypt. These plagues tease out the problems hidden under the surface of the characters, unusual circumstances forcing protagonists and those around them to discover then confront desires and issues from deep within. Joe Baumann is a force of nature, and his collection is imaginative, heartfelt, and brilliant, and an absolute must-have.

—Aura Martin
author of *Butterflies Over Flame*

The Plagues

Stories

Joe Baumann

Cornerstone Press
Stevens Point, Wisconsin

Cornerstone Press, Stevens Point, Wisconsin 54481
Copyright © 2023 Joe Baumann
www.uwsp.edu/cornerstone

Printed in the United States of America by
Point Print and Design Studio, Stevens Point, Wisconsin

Library of Congress Control Number: 2022944564
ISBN: 979-8-9861447-7-1

Cornerstone Press titles are produced in courses and internships offered by the Department of English at the University of Wisconsin–Stevens Point.

DIRECTOR & PUBLISHER   EXECUTIVE EDITOR
Dr. Ross K. Tangedal   Jeff Snowbarger

SENIOR EDITORS
Lexie Neeley, Monica Swinick, Kala Buttke

PRESS STAFF
Alyssa Bronk, Grace Dahl, Patrick Fogarty, Angela Green, Cal Henkens, Brett Hill, Ryan Jensen, Julia Kaufman, Hunter Kiesow, Adam King, Amanda Leibham, Maria Scherer, Abbi Wasielewski

To my friends and family

Also by Joe Baumann:

Sing With Me at the Edge of Paradise

I Know You're Out There Somewhere

Hot Lips

Terrarium

Ivory Children

Stories

Transubstantiation

It began at the public pool, right when my sister Kathleen's best friend Meggie shot herself down the largest of three waterslides, the pond-scum-green plastic tubing coiled like a snake. Meggie shrieked as her body shot along the curves, voice echoing through the cavern of plastic. Her arms flailed like noodles as she splashed into the three-foot deep wading pool. Brian Munson, who I'd been in love with since I was in seventh grade (he was a year older), stood watch, his red lifeguard's swim trunks short enough to reveal the thickness of his thighs. I was lying nearby on a chaise, smearing sunscreen on my chest, which had finally started to take on some definition since I'd started doing two hundred pushups every day, my gawking stares at Brian hidden behind my sunglasses. I saw the furrow of his bushy eyebrows and the languid, careful way he brought his lifeguard whistle to his bright, wet lips when he noticed the blood.

At first, it was hard to tell that what followed Meggie was, in fact, blood. After she splashed down into the pool, limbs akimbo, the water started to change. Instead of the pearly blue chuff that normally spewed from the curved lip of the slide, the water was tinged a darker something that at first looked purplish like a bruise but then turned bright red, gushing like the spazzy flow in a Tarantino movie when someone's head gets chopped off. Brian Munson moved in Meggie's direction, whistle poised in his mouth, fifty-inch rescue tube tucked under one bronzed arm. His abs twitched and as I watched I felt at my own stomach, not quite as muscle-lined but not globbed over with fat, either. Had he ever paid me a single drop of attention in his life, I'd like to think Brian would at least be appreciative, if not equally attracted to, the leanness of my physique.

Brian's dashing in her direction made Meggie look around, and when she saw the blood rushing toward her from the slide's mouth she screamed and began hopping, shoving her hands through the water as though she could send the thick muck back in the direction from which it came. It took a minute before anyone else noticed the blood, which started jetting from the other two slides; a boy, maybe nine or ten, barely meeting the height requirement for the open-air white slide, came shooting down and found himself slathered in the stuff as if he had been cast as Carrie and had just filmed the prom scene. He stood and guffawed at himself, fingers spread like a duck's webbed feet, globulin and plasma sticky between them.

Pandemonium spread quickly, as though a turd had been found. Blood spewed from the mushroom spray fountain; it seeped out from beneath the buoyant lily pads bobbing under the dual cargo nets. In the kiddie section, the blurpy spumes of water that shot up from jets embedded in the concrete like streams from pissing angel statues turned into waggling crimson tongues. Parents gathered their kids; teens gawked and shrieked. Brian Munson dragged Meggie out of the way right as my sister splashed down behind her, her body filmed with so much blood she looked as though she had been turned inside out. I stood, feeling the tingle of the sun on my back and shoulders, and reached out for my sister's hand while Brian helped Meggie from the pool. Lifeguards everywhere were blaring their whistles, hauling frumpy fifty-year-olds from the lap lanes, screeching for giddy boys to get the fuck out of the water. My sister was frozen, the blood thick and copper-smelling. Meggie shivered. Brian blinked at me, staring with pseudo-recognition. Among the din and confusion, I felt a flutter, an excitement. He asked who I was.

By the time Meggie and Kathleen were cleaned up enough that I could haul them into the old coughing station wagon that my sister and I shared, the blood had spread. Red liquid oozed from our sink faucets when I tried to pour a glass of water; Meggie shrieked from the hall bath and said that when the toilet refilled it looked like a bowl of spiked punch. I turned on the television and the newscasts were agog with the story, reporters googly-eyed in front of the Missouri River, stained a deep copper; at the Illinois border, the Muddy Mississippi looked like a burst of Kool-Aid. At the Howard Bend treatment plant workers were clumped outside, staring down at the gush of churning bloody refuse. Neither my sister nor Meggie could rinse the crusts from their skin because the showerheads spewed out clotted red liquid the consistency of corn syrup. When Kathleen started crying, I sat her down, a tropical-themed towel wrapped around her just to be safe. I wet a paper towel with my own saliva and wiped at her bloodstained elbows.

She and Meggie mumbled to one another, but I wasn'tlistening, not to them nor to the gray-eyed, gray-haired anchorman on the television. I was thinking of Brian Munson, who had peeled off his sunglasses after I told him my name. He'd squinted and then shut his eyes, reaching his hand up to pinch at the bridge of his nose, as if the gushes of blood coming from the pool's filtration system were a minor frustration that he would be charged with fixing. Then he blinked, his eyes wide and owlish, and asked me if we had been in the same pre-calculus class. I nodded, then admitted I had only been a sophomore.

"Too smart for my own good," I managed to say.

Brian Munson had smiled at that, and the warmth in my chest had gone volcanic. Around me, the din raged, mothers in one-piece bathing suits grabbing up their traumatized, blood-stained children, teens laughing and pointing, the elderly shaking with fear, but I could focus only on the pinch of flesh between Brian's pecs, where the muscle ribbed up snug against his breastbone like strips of Velcro.

He'd offered to help get the girls home, but then his supervisor came thundering along the pool, a pot-bellied man wearing a visor and blue polo shirt stained with trails of sweat at the chest and armpits. He wore flip flops, and his toes hung over them. He screamed for Brian to join the other lifeguards at an emergency meeting. Brian, with what I thought was a gawk of longing in my direction, watched us leave, shrugging his bronzed shoulders and waving goodbye, whistle in hand.

Bottled water disappeared from shelves with frantic, phantasmagoric speed. When people realized their other sources—water fountains, garden hoses, soda machines, sprinkler systems (many of which spritzed otherwise lush lawns with a pasty layer of red)—had been contaminated by the transformation, flocks of the harried and terrified rushed to grocery stores and gas stations, snarling and fighting over every plastic-wrapped twenty-four pack of Aquafina and

Fiji, jabbing elbows over gallons of distilled water, throwing hooks and crosses as they scrambled for bags of ice. They slaughtered the sports drink aisles and grabbed up all the juice, both bottled and concentrate. Cooking became a problem, as did washing clothes and going to the bathroom. FEMA was called. The National Reserve showed up. We all learned the word *hydrologist*, as top water scientists were shipped in to figure out what the heck was going on. They blinked into cameras and tried to sound professional, but the message was clear: no one knew.

During a house fire three streets from ours, firefighters tried to access the nearest hydrant and found themselves in possession of a gushing spume of blood. It took down the flames, finally, but left the house turned into a cavernous blob. Wild animals stalked the area, frustrated by the metallic smell and the lack of flesh to gnaw. The blood crusted over and the insurance company said to just knock the whole thing down and start anew.

Kathleen and I watched tv, sweating and stinking up our nasty, hot house; our parents hated that the air conditioning unit dripped blood, which coagulated in a gunky pond on the side of the house, so they commanded we turn it off and rely on fans and our swimsuits for temperate survival. We decided we hated them, and we were glad when they left for work without bothering us with good morning kisses and hugs and waffles.

One afternoon, two weeks after the incident at the pool, my phone buzzed. Meggie and Kathleen were stuffed in the basement, practicing field hockey moves, working on traps, leads, and passes in the comfort of the cool, earthy dark. I could periodically hear the scrape of their sticks against the epoxied floor, the whack of the ball when it hit the wall. I was lying on the couch, body sticky like flypaper, ignoring an episode of *Judge Judy*. My throat was dry already, my one rationed bottle of water two-thirds gone.

The number was unfamiliar, but the text message accompanying it, blaring out on my old iPhone's screen like a beacon, was clear: *Hey, it's Brian. You bored?*

A jolt rippled my stomach and my inner cheeks soured. Surely he had the wrong number; we had not spoken since the day at the pool, and I had no idea how he'd even managed to track down my phone number in the first place. Brian Munson and I barely crossed paths at school; he swung through the oeuvres of the basketball team, the baseball players, and the jazz band (I snuck into a concert last fall, sitting toward the back, and stared at him, trim and tight in a cummerbund and white button-down, lips pressed thoughtfully around the mouthpiece of a clarinet; he stood for a solo during *Mission to Moscow* and I felt my throat chug and leap). I, on the other hand, was mired in a reputation that extended no further than my prowess with numbers and a weak connection to the theatre geeks after I stumbled into the role of Snoopy for the production of *You're a Good Man, Charlie Brown!*

I stared at Brian's message.

Oh hey, I typed. *What's up?*

I wanted to add: *You know who this is, right?*

He appeared at the front door twenty minutes later; I swung it open before he could knock or press the doorbell so Kathleen and Meggie, still thwacking away in the basement, wouldn't hear. He looked startled, hand poised to poke at the bell, and when he saw me, a sheepish grin bubbled on his lips. Brian was wearing a blue tank top so tight it looked like it had been shellacked to his skin, but his glaring white board shorts swallowed his lower body. A pancake-thin strip of gold skin winked out between the two, and I had to resist letting my gaze settle there.

"You ready?" he said.

"Umm." I peered over my shoulder, toward the kitchen and the door to the basement, then looked back. "Yeah."

Brian's truck, a lumbering red thing, was parked on the curb, one tire pressing against the tangle of grass that my father had let grow out of control ever since the appearance of the blood. The front yard was dotted with dandelions, better in comparison to the back, where my father had set up huge white barrels for collecting rain, which fortunately still fell as water. When a strong enough storm ran through, my mother boiled it so she could make pasta at night and coffee in the morning.

"You drive?" Brian said when we had closed ourselves into the truck's cab, the doors squealing as we shut them in unison.

"Yeah," I said. "I got my license a few months ago." I flicked a thumb toward the station wagon, ashamed of its peeling blue paint and cracked rear windshield. "My sister and I share."

"Just wondering. You want a beer?" Brian glanced toward the bench seat behind us, black leather shot full of holes where yellow sponge oozed out, a Styrofoam cooler was sweating in its center.

"Oh. Sure, I guess. Is it safe?"

Brian shrugged as I reached back. "Just hide it if you see a cop car. I never get pulled over."

The can was cold and slick, the condensation a shock against my palm. I stared at the blue and white lettering for a moment before popping it open with a hearty, yeasty hiss. I'd never drank beer before but wasn't surprised that Brian had somehow managed to secure it. I had heard about plenty of wild weekend parties that the athletes and cheerleaders threw, the gossip and stories of dancing and chugging and strip poker growing out of control like wildfire as they spread through the halls at school, hyperbolized by word of mouth to the point that the parties sounded more like Roman orgies than high school keggers.

I took a deep sip of the beer, my tongue and lips tingling and recoiling at the bitter, bison taste. I clenched my teeth as I swallowed so I wouldn't belch it back up or hack. I could feel Brian's eyes sliding from the road to me and back, a pinch of smile settling in the dimple of his right cheek.

"Where are we going?" I asked, nestling the beer between my legs.

Brian shrugged. "There's a neat patch of land near the river. It's usually pretty nice there. Quiet."

"Bloody," I said.

"Yeah, I guess it is, now."

"It's weird, you know?"

"It's the end of the world!" Brian shouted, releasing the wheel and waving his hands toward the windshield. "That's what the pastor at my mom's church says, anyway.."

"You go to church?"

"Not really, except on Christmas and Easter. But my mom subjects me to a lengthy rehash of the sermon every week." He reattached his hands to the wheel, ten and two. Thick veins jutted along his knuckle bones. "What about you?"

I shook my head. "My parents are atheists."

"I asked about you, not your parents."

I felt a heat bloom in my cheeks and took another sip of the beer. My mouth felt coated in aluminum and my tongue still wanted to raise high hellish rebellion, but I swallowed with greater ease than the first sip.

"I'm not sure what I think."

"What about the beer, at least?"

"It's good," I said.

Brian laughed. "You don't have to pretend," he said as he signaled to merge onto the interstate and glanced over his shoulder as he pulled the truck into traffic. "It's okay if you haven't drank before, you know."

"I have."

"Okay. I'm just saying, it's no big deal."

I sighed. "How could you tell?"

"Everyone looks grossed out when they take their first sip of beer. Especially that stuff. It's like nine dollars for a twelve-pack."

"Is that cheap?"

Brian laughed again, a sharp chirp of noise, more like a dog's bark than anything else. But it was loose and free, absent any malice or mocking. The natural frown of his forehead vanished, his mouth opening to reveal Crest commercial teeth. His Adam's apple bobbed like a thrashing buoy. He reached out his right hand and planted it atop my left shoulder, fingers squeezing against my flesh. It made me feel small, tinier than the four inches shorter I was than Brian. He looked godlike, the kind of hero who would be cast in gold and placed at the center of a Greek temple.

"Let's just say it's a good deal." He looked at me again, long enough that I had to look back. I wished I was wearing sunglasses or that he wasn't. He could see right through me, but I couldn't do the same to him.

The clearing was well-hidden. After easing the truck off the interstate at the Fifth Street exit, Brian negotiated the roads sweeping toward Main Street. We crossed a pair of old cobblestone streets, jostling in the cab of the truck while the beer cans in their melting ice sloshed in the back seat. Then Brian slid us past the public parking lots that lined the riverfront in patient asphalt squares and swung onto a nearly-invisible gravel road cutting into a thicket of trees. We rumbled for half a mile, red flashes of the bloodied Missouri River glinting through the trees. The road was so narrow that branches thwacked against the roof and windows, clacking like drumsticks against the glass. Eventually the strip of road ended in a bulbous cul-de-sac next to a patch of green grass and a picnic table. We hauled ourselves from the truck. Brian grabbed the cooler and led the way, bypassing the table with its rotted-looking planks. He marched until we were ten feet from the water, then he plopped down the cooler and, without a word, tossed himself on the grass in a long, languorous repose. I sat down on the other side of the ice chest, cross-legged.

Brian crunched himself up and tossed open the cooler, fishing out a can.

"You ready for another one?"

I could already feel the tingly buzz of the first beer, its unpleasant, rank taste covering every surface of my mouth. I shook my head and rattled my can, which was still a third full. "Not quite."

Brian shrugged and popped open his can, a spray of foam spattering on the thick swatch of flesh between his thumb and forefinger. He stuck his mouth around his skin and my eyes rested on his lips as they pulsed and sucked. When he was done, he laid down again, beer can nestled in the grass, hands cradling the back of his head as he stared up at the sky, silent.

Neither of us spoke for a long while. My eyes wandered, to the treetops, the grass in front of me, the water. The river was cakey on its banks, clotted with blood and soil. A few dead fish floated on the water's surface, which barely seemed to move; the thickness had slowed its flow to a spidery crawl. Strangely, there was no smell. I'd become accustomed to the sharp blood scent that hovered over everything now, as if a slaughterhouse was nearby, and the lack of the heavy metal aroma left my nose tingly with the sweetness of the greenery surrounding us.

I finished my beer and fished in the cooler for another. My head was a little swimmy, the edges of my vision blurred like the outer edges of an old television. Brian wobbled into my sight, his creamy, bronze skin electric and bright against the grass. I still had no idea what he wanted with me. I popped open my beer and drank deeply.

"It's an acquired taste," Brian said when I was done. He hauled himself up and rested his weight on his splayed palms, arms shot out behind him so the lean muscles of his triceps popped. "You seem to be acquiring it quickly."

"I'm a fast learner," I said. My tongue felt loose, unhooked from the bottom of my mouth. I grinned.

Brian nodded. "I figured you would be." After a moment of silence, he slurped from his beer and gestured toward the river, waving his beer can so the bottom flashed toward the blooded water. "You never said what you think of all this."

I considered, nodding my head as if I was deep in thought, though I was really distracted by the widening gap between Brian's shirt and his shorts, which had ridden up his thighs.

His hair, blonde and spiky, dissipated like a breeze as it trailed up his legs.

"It's very, umm. Biblical."

He snorted. "Okay, yeah."

"But not so scientific."

"Things aren't usually both, are they?"

"Nope." I took another deep swig of beer.

"May want to slow down there, tiger."

The word *tiger* emerged from his mouth like a soft puff of air, a sweet pillow of sound. I shut my eyes and rewound the moment, focusing in on Brian's lips, their redness amplified and slickened by the beer. In the darkness of my shut eyes, little bursts of purple and yellow spat out. I felt myself sway like I was listening to a slow dance number.

"You okay?"

"Never better." I opened my eyes, wide. Brian was sitting up straight now, one hand on the cooler between us. I set my free hand there, too. Only a few inches separated our fingers. I wanted some magic to shrink the cooler and bring our hands together. I knew it would take only one touch, one zap of skin-to-skin contact for Brian's walls to come down. We would tumble together, Brian raking at the back of my head and my hips as our lips met, his warm, experienced fingers in control. He would whip me onto the ground, and I would feel his weight push me deep into the soil.

He took his hand from the cooler. Then he tugged at the straps of his tank top and pulled it off.

Brian laid back down, the muscles of his chest and stomach stretched out like they were made of putty. His hip bones pressed against his skin like door handles. I looked toward the river so I didn't gawk.

Soon, Brian's breath had gone regular, a tight wheezy noise escaping his lips. His shirt was bunched on the grass, pressed beneath his head and hands. I could see the stubbly hair beneath his armpits. With each inhalation his ribs expanded, the muscles that gripped his sides like large stretching bite marks. I finished my beer and opened another, then pulled off my own shirt. We were arranged in the shade of treetops, so the sun glanced off my skin indirectly. I felt droopy compared to Brian; his body was easy and lithe, his muscles lean and effortlessly tight. When I laid myself down, I squeezed strength into my biceps, felt them fill with the tingly pain of contraction, little blurbs of lactic acid finding their way into the fibers. My stomach, unlike Brian's, looked like a gurgling tub, the crater of my abdomen filled with movable flesh.

I closed my eyes and the world tilted beneath me, swaying hard and fast and with enough strength that I thought I would tumble, be pitched to the side so I crashed against the cooler and smashed into Brian, our bodies connecting just long enough for me to feel the sizzle of his flesh before I catapulted off the planet and swirled into outer space. When I opened my eyes the sky above me swung and heaved, the sights around me—maple trees, periwinkles, the cavern of blue-and-white above—jostled and then came back into focus. I drank from my beer, letting the fuzzy liquid linger in my mouth.

I peered over the cooler toward Brian. His body was slender and calm, breathing still regular. I could see that, beneath his sunglasses, his eyes were shut and his eyelashes locked against one another. He looked regal, like someone you'd see photographed on the deck of a yacht, cradled in an advertisement for Ralph Lauren or Tommy Hilfiger, the ocean lapping at the edges of the frame.

I finished the beer, hardly tasting it as I swallowed. Then I stood, rickety and drunk; I had to lean one hand on the cooler to haul myself up. I didn't know what I was doing, didn't ask myself why or think ahead. Instead, I stepped around to Brian's side of the cooler and knelt next to him, feeling a pinch above my groin, my bladder screaming to be emptied.

His body was so close, his delicate face with its charging cheekbones and blemish-free skin radiating a honeyed smell. I leaned closer and listened to the workings of his body, the chuff of air wheezing in and out through his pursed lips. His skin buzzed with life, the little blond hairs on his arms and legs swaying. He popped like a car engine recently cut. My face hovered before his, and before I knew it my lips were aimed at his, only a few inches separating the two of us. We were close enough that I could see the craters of pores along the sides of his nose.

The rhythm of his breath hitched, then stopped. I looked, and his eyes were open.

The lenses of his sunglasses tinted his eyes a blackish-blue. Everything inside me changed, my bones tumbling into a clacking pile, muscles stiffening with rigor mortis, blood spiking with a tingly pain. I felt the strain in my thighs from squatting for so long, knees pulsating with discomfort. My breath went loud and hard and noxious from the fungal influence of the beers. My throat felt clogged.

I kissed him. Then I pulled back, stumbling onto my feet.

Brian didn't move. He stared. Nothing about him was any different except for the glare of his eyes meeting mine. I slipped across the grass.

He turned onto his side, head propped up by his right arm, which was tripoded into the grass. Brian said nothing, but his mouth was working, hitching, as if he couldn't make up his mind. He blinked over and over like an expensive digital camera taking dozens of high-resolution photographs. Every second that passed stole some tiny bit of me, like my skin cells were flaking away, transforming me into something new. My ears rang with an unpleasant tinnitus.

The noise of the water filled my ears: gunky, lapping, sludgy. Before I knew what I was doing I was prying off my shoes, unfurling my socks, and leaving them humped like snowballs in the grass. Then I was off to the river, nonplussed by the kaleidoscope of color and the dizziness that invaded my brain, a lightheaded feeling like I hadn't taken a breath in years.

Brian finally yelled out, some wordless noise of either regret or fear or anger or wonder, but I was too beer-soaked to know which. The smell of the blood finally hit me as I reached the edge of the river. Its surface was slick and crimson like Brian's wet lips. Had I been sober I'd have hesitated, probably tripped and belly-flopped my way in, but I didn't slow at all, not even when Brian cried out again. I leapt, taking the small plummet standing straight up so my feet hit first, the blood warm and thick as syrup. I felt the twisting, turning world pulsing and clawing at me, working hard to turn me into something new before I broke the surface. My lungs ached, and as I floated upward, I closed my eyes and prayed and hoped, wished the blood would carry me away to a place that I could understand.

Amphibians

When she walked through the door, Marle tried to recall the last time someone had checked into the motel after three a.m. By that hour it was usually safe for him to pull up PornHub on his phone. When he heard the yawning of the door opening Marle was eight minutes into a MMF threesome, two frat boys going to town on a bronzed co-ed, their flat torsos flexing and expanding. He was paying particular attention to the blond, his stomach dusted with fine, golden hairs that glinted under the heavy lighting, hips covered in sloped muscle from plenty of bicycle crunches. Marle hit pause and silenced his phone, and in the scramble to do so smacked his knee against the counter's underside as he stood.

She was wearing a neon green rain slicker, hood pinched over her straggly black hair even though the air was dry as a wheezy throat; the night sky was an onyx blanket pocked with stars, the incandescent glow of nearby Vegas humming on the horizon. But the woman somehow looked wet, as though she'd run through the tepid fountain out front. Her face was streaked with mascara as though she'd been crying and, although Marle was no make-up expert, even he could tell she'd done a piss-poor job of blending her foundation along the jawline, where her flesh shifted from a powdery peach color to something more corpse-like.

"Good evening," Marle managed, keeping one hand below the counter to adjust the erection wilting beneath his shorts. "How can I help you?"

"You have a room?" the woman said. Her voice was breathless, eyes wide with need.

"Sure," Marle said. "Single or double?"

"Doesn't matter," she said. "As long as it's second floor. Away from the pool, please."

"No problem." Tuesday nights weren't much popular, especially this late. Half the guests paid by the hour and would have gone home by now.

"Just one night?" he asked, turning to the corkboard of keys behind him.

She nodded.

He plucked one of the keys and set it on the counter. "We'll put you in twenty-one. It's actually just upstairs above the office here. You'll take the first stairwell to your right when you go out."

"Thanks," she said. She reached under the slicker and extracted a pool of crinkled bills, tossing them on the counter. "I don't need change."

Before Marle could say a word, the girl had grabbed up the key and dashed out the door.

By the time it slammed shut, the first frogs had appeared.

He heard them before he saw them, their deep burpy noises reminding Marle of summers in Louisiana at his aunt's shotgun house in Breaux Bridge, where the spitty night heat was filled with the throaty noises of reptilian and insect life burbling in Bayou Teche. He and his aunt would sit on the front porch, drinking sweet tea. They didn't speak much, their bodies collecting filmy sweat that no amount of cold tea could stave off. The symphony of noise helped them sleep when they finally dragged themselves inside, Marle to the pull-out sofa in the living room and his aunt to the bedroom.

The noise wasn't as sharp inside the motel office. He made a mental note of his video's title for later recovery and walked to the door. The parking lot was a dark pool of nothing, even the butter-colored fountain an indistinct blob past the stairs.

He opened the door, letting the chilly fume of Nevada summer air splash his face. A rusting white Cadillac was parked at an uncomfortable diagonal, one tire bumped up on the curb. It obscured half of the fountain, so Marle still couldn't see the frogs, though he could hear their steady rhythmic belches.

He stepped into the lot. A dozen fat, slimy bullfrogs were sitting on the rim of the fountain, amphibian feet drooping against the concrete lip. Their deep ribbiting continued and Marle stood watching, not sure what for. Finally, one of the larger frogs shifted its weight and plopped into the fountain with a soft splash and the dull thrall they'd cast on Marle snapped. He shook his head. The frogs were certainly a curiosity, and had, in Marle's memory, never made an appearance near the motel before—he wasn't actually sure bullfrogs were native to Nevada—but he thought little of them and slipped back into the office.

The clock behind the check-in counter read three twenty-two; Marle's shift ended at six, when Becky, his overripe manager with blonde hair fried by one too many permanents, would hobble in (bad left knee; she claimed she'd suffered an ACL tear during a college softball game when she slid into second base, though Marle suspected that she'd slipped and fallen in, say, the prepackaged snack aisle at the nearby Vons). Becky was eternally sweat-stained, her body apparently having never adapted to the arid Vegas atmosphere; her blue polo shirts looked like they had been tie-dyed, dark loops of sweat etching their way out from the underarms, across the lower back, and, most conspicuously, snarling from beneath her generous chest. He knew Becky scheduled their shift swap early enough that the handful of low-rent businessmen whose companies wouldn't pay for a nicer hotel closer to the dazzling glitz of Las Vegas checked out under her watch rather than his, as if her "expertise" (her word) was somehow more impressive than his own ability to punch up their bills as they rushed to get on the road, ties askew, foreheads already moist.

Which meant he only had two and a half hours to go before he could crash into his apartment and sleep. Marle pulled his phone from his pocket. He would have to be careful, though, and watch with one eye toward the door, the other admiring the glistening, flexing muscles on the screen.

The desk phone brayed out a tinny whine. Marle leapt from his chair, knocking his other knee as his phone clattered down screen-first.

"Fuck! Ow." Marle took a deep breath, then plucked up the phone on the second ring. He'd never actually had to answer it before, so he let silence hang in the air for a second before saying, "Hello?"

"Is this the front desk?" It was the woman, her voice still trapped in that choppy, hyperventilating cadence.

"Yes. Can I help you?"

"Do you have room service?"

Marle choked down a laugh. The office didn't even have free coffee. He told her no. "But there are a few vending machines just to the right of your room. You'd have seen them on your way up. I'm not sure how long ago they were stocked, so I'd be wary of the—"

"I can't leave the room."

"Oh. Well. I don't think there's any pizza places open yet."

"Can you hear them?" she said, her voice dropping to a low whisper.

"Who?"

"Don't pretend. I know you can. They're so loud."

"Excuse me?"

She hung up.

The throb of noise, like the snores emanating from a gallery of sleeping old men, rose like a tidal wave. He left his downturned phone on the counter and walked to the door, still a reflective black that showed more of his own glinting reflection than anything outside. With a hitch of hesitation, he pushed it open.

The noise was deafening, a choral ode of frog sounds chiming in a syncopated round. Once again, Marle heard them before he saw them, and he nearly took a step, glancing down at the last second. He leapt back. Not only had the frogs multiplied, they'd moved, a gaggle of them strewn across the sidewalk in front of the office, a heavy drizzle of amphibious bodies leading from the fountain to the motel. They congregated in clusters on the concrete in pod-like formations all the way to the corrugated stairs leading to the second floor. There must have been thirty or forty, ranging in size from tennis ball to catcher's mitt.

Marle wasn't afraid of frogs, but he backed up and shut the door and then turned the lock. He plopped down in his squeaky chair behind the counter and took a deep breath, waiting for the wave of blood thumping through his temples to subside. Then he plucked up the phone and dialed room twenty-one.

"You looked for them, didn't you?"

"What is happening?"

"You saw them."

"Yes."

The phone crackled as the woman exhaled.

"More of them are coming."

The prophetic sting in her voice sent a thrummy shiver up from the base of his spine to Marle's shoulders. "Where are they coming from? Do we even have these things in Las Vegas?"

"We have everything in Las Vegas."

"I didn't mean metaphorically."

"*Lithobates catesbeianus.*"

"Is that a spell or something? Are you chanting Latin?"

"That's their scientific name."

"Oh," Marle said. "Is that helpful information?"

"Knowledge is always helpful."

"So how about where they came from? What are they doing?"

"You should come up here," the woman said.

"What?"

"You'll be safe here."

"They're just frogs."

"There're going to be a lot of frogs."

"How do you know? How did you know? Is this why you wanted a second floor room?"

"You should come up here."

"Does this have something to do with you wearing a poncho?"

"You'd better hurry. Before it's too late."

She hung up. Marle picked up his phone: still not quite four.

Outside, the frogs had multiplied. Marle took a deep breath. A pungent reptilian smell gathered in his nostrils; it reminded him of the beach mixed with something sulfurous. He stepped onto the sidewalk. Among the clot of frogs were clear bits of concrete like flagstones on a path. Marle tiptoed from one free space to another. The frogs didn't notice him, sitting in their burpy groups like disaffected teenagers ignoring the world around them. They had yet to colonize the stairs, so when Marle reached the first step he paused for a short breather. He had once played basketball, but the most vigorous physical activity he'd engaged in for the last several months were the various masturbatory efforts he put in before or after his shifts. He was pretty sure he'd read somewhere that sex could burn hundreds of calories per hour, but he was also pretty sure such an accomplishment required a partner and for it to actually last an hour. He'd gone vegetarian and given up soda, though, which kept his waistline trim. As he panted on the stairs, he told himself he'd start doing pushups and a few planks before bed.

He stopped in front of the door to room twenty-one. She swung it open before he had a chance to rap his knuckles against the chippy red paint. The girl was no longer wearing the bloated poncho, and Marle could see he'd mistaken her for younger than she was. Her face was lined with age, small wrinkles nipping at the corners of her lips and eyes, but they gave her a look of rounded, aware intelligence. She was a collection of sharp angles: cheekbones that jutted from her skin, nose clipped like an arrowhead, chin pointed out like a coat hook. Her eyes were a supernatural blue, like a bottle of Bombay Sapphire.

She had dried off and hardly resembled the version self that looked like she'd been boiled just before first walking into the office. Her makeup was a smooth, singular mask.

The woman said nothing. She brushed past Marle and leaned over the railing of the walkway, peering down for two seconds, head turning to the right and then left and then back again before she stood up straight and backed into the room, fastening one hand around his bicep with a grip so tight Marle felt himself bruising. She yanked him inside.

Most of the motel's rooms were plagued by a fish tank smell, as though they'd flooded and been left to dry without cleanup. But the woman must have sprayed something because Marle's nose was assaulted by lavender and jasmine. Both queen beds were undisturbed, the itchy, flimsy floral-print bedspreads smooth. Marle couldn't see a bag or suitcase or any personal belongings, and other than the fact that the buzzy bathroom light was on and the Gideon bible sat open on the small disk of a side table, there was no evidence that the woman had done much settling in.

"Shut the door," she ordered him. Marle did, and then watched as she flung herself into the room's lone chair and propped herself in front of the bible. She started reading.

"So," he said. "You, uh, know what's going on with the frogs?"

Her eyes remained locked on the bible. She flicked the page.

"That depends on what you mean by 'know'," she said.

"I'm not sure what I mean by that. But you seem to know something."

She blinked at him.

"What's your name?" Marle said.

"You first."

"I'm Marle."

"Weird name."

"Weird parents, I guess."

"You guess?"

"They died when I was six. Lived with an aunt then. She died of emphysema."

"And then?"

"Foster parents until I turned eighteen."

"Rough childhood."

"I survived."

"And here you are."

Marle shrugged.

"I'm Rebecca."

"And what's your story?"

"I don't have one."

"Everyone has a story."

"Well, mine's short. I'm here."

"Why are you here?"

"What do you mean?"

Marle pointed toward the bible. "The frogs. You knew they were coming."

"Anyone who looked hard enough could have known that."

"What does that mean?"

"The clues are all in here," she said, stabbing at the bible.

"The clues that they would come today?"

"Well," she said, leaning back as if in defeat. "It's not quite that pinpoint accurate. But it wasn't any of the other likely days, so it had to be this one."

"And why here? What does God want to plague Las Vegas for? Heck, we're not even really in Vegas. I'm pretty sure this is unincorporated county."

When she didn't answer, Marle said, "So what will the frogs do?"

"Do?"

"I mean, they were a plague, right? They're just, I don't know, sitting there. They didn't attack me or anything."

"When did you last read about frogs mauling anyone, Marle?"

"That's kind of my point. What'll they do?"

"Pretty much die and be stinky."

"Sounds crummy for the frogs."

"Also crummy for us."

"So why are you here then?"

"Huh?"

Marle sat on the end of the closest bed. "You're here."

"I am."

"Why? If you knew the frogs would come, why did you come, too?"

Rebecca frowned, her face swallowed by a maze of wrinkled flesh. Marle's bonked knees pulsed with sudden pain. She leaned back in her chair, turned her feet inward pigeon-toe style, and let out a long exhale like a wheezy balloon farting out the last of its air.

"I don't know, Marle."

"You don't know?"

"I was not here and then I was."

Marle frowned. "I'm not so keen on riddles."

She raised her hands like a cornered suspect. "I don't know what to tell you."

"Didn't you drive here?"

"That is my car downstairs, yes."

"And you don't know how you ended up here? So it was like some Jesus take the wheel thing?"

"I suppose it was."

Marle stood. The room felt damp, like a gust of steam had snarled out of the bathroom and coated the walls, the drapery, the scratchy bedspread. Beads of sweat broke along his hairline and under his arms. His throat went dry.

"You look ill, Marle."

Marle's head was spinning, feeling doughy, like he'd just been punched in the temple. "What did you do to me?"

Rebecca didn't so much as glance at him. "What makes you think I did something to you, Marle?"

"I don't—"

"What, Marle?"

"What is going on?"

"The Lord works in mysterious ways." She stood, passing Marle and pulling the curtains apart so she could peer through. "They haven't reached the second floor yet."

Marle went to the window and glanced out into the prunish night. The sky languored with stars and wisps of cirrus clouds like white paint streaks. Below, on the grimed parking lot, the bumpy bodies of frogs were scattered across the asphalt.

"I love a good sunrise," Rebecca said.

"The view here isn't great."

"No offense, Marle, but nothing here seems that great."

"I won't disagree."

"So why are you here?"

"Huh?"

"What are you doing here?"

"I'm working."

She smiled, a sad grimace. "I mean, long term."

"Is this some kind of weird intervention? Who are you?"

"Just asking a question. I like to know what people want out of their lives."

"This is all very strange," Marle said.

"I'm just curious if working the night shift at a one-star motel in the middle of nowhere is what your dreams are made of."

"Ouch."

"Honesty, not brutality."

"What about brutal honesty?"

"Come on, Marle. Really think about it. What do you want?"

Marle opened his mouth, but no words came out.

After high school he left Louisiana, convinced there was something better, and Vegas seemed as better as anywhere else, and he had just enough money saved up from working at a Chili's to pay for a bus ticket and put down a month's rent on a ramshackle studio apartment in Henderson. He nabbed a job at the Applebee's off Interstate 15, mostly feeding truckers and groups of cheap-ass college kids who were road tripping into Vegas. Then the franchise was hit with some serious health code violations and then lost its liquor license when one of the bartenders served an entire cadre of undercover teens working for the ABC. The bartender didn't card a single one, and without the promise of two-dollar margaritas and half-off pints after nine, customers petered out. Marle applied for all the jobs he could, finally landing at the motel after a quick, stupid interview with Becky where he was asked three questions: Can you work through the night? Do you have any felony convictions? Can you read and write?

"Do you want," Rebecca said, "to be one of the men on your phone?"

"What?"

"On your phone. I heard it when I first came in."

Marle felt his face flare.

"It's okay, Marle. Perfectly normal behavior. Maybe not while you're on the clock, but that's not for me to judge. The adult entertainment industry is huge for a reason."

"Um."

"But no," she said, shaking her head. "You don't want to be one of those guys." She narrowed her eyes. "You want to be with one of them."

"I don't—"

"You don't have to pretend."

"I'm not pretending anything."

"Non-admission is a kind of pretending."

"Who are you?"

"I already told you my name."

"That's not what I meant."

"It's all I can give."

Marle tapped on the window. "You brought them, didn't you? The frogs."

"I certainly did not."

"Are you God?"

"Are you a believer?"

"You keep answering my questions with questions."

"Is that god-like to you?"

Marle moaned. "I have to go back to the office. I can't get fired."

"You won't. We have plenty of time to talk about your interests."

Marle took a step toward the door. "You keep changing. First you're timid and afraid, and now you're convinced I want to, what, screw a guy?"

"Well, that's a brusque way of putting it, Marle. Love and sex are different. Though you're right that they're related."

Marle let out a frustrated howl and drew the door open. The frogs began their chorus, the thrumming plosive noise chiming up as though they'd been waiting for an audience.

"No!" Rebecca yelled. "Shut the door!"

"Why?" Marle said. "You're afraid of them, aren't you?"

"Just close it."

"Okay," Marle said, curling his hand around the door's thickness. He stepped out onto the second-story walkway and pushed the door, closing off room twenty-one behind him.

The dry heat of morning was already stirring up from the ground; steam chuffed up out of the grate in the parking lot's dipped center and evaporated into the scorched warmth. Marle looked over the balcony: the frogs were everywhere, covering the parking lot like a field of chaff. He could see over the line of Floribunda rose bushes to the smeary, empty highway: the frogs had begun an exodus into the dusty roadway, a trail of bodies dotting a line from the motel to the asphalt, where they would surely be squashed to gutsy blasts by unprepared motorists. That, according to Rebecca, seemed to be their fate: to stink and die and squelch and rot, bothersome in their odious death.

Marle turned and made for the stairs, passing the sallow illumination of the vending machines. Rebecca did not follow him outside.

The frogs still hadn't made any attempts at the second floor, but they were a thick mass blocking the sidewalk. Marle stopped at the landing halfway up and looked over the railing. He could see I-15, a few cars dotting the horizon, their high beams cutting through the berry-blue darkness to illuminate rocks, the center lane lines, the bumps of the shoulder's rumble strip. The frogs were lined up at the motel's entrance. He watched a few of them hop into the road; some had already made the trek, spread out like infectious disease. As one car passed, he saw the blurred, fudgy outline of a squashed frog, its body gushing out its innards in a wet splat of oozy blood and intestines.

He could almost hear Rebecca's voice in his ear, as if she was standing behind him, whispering the words to a song. Her question, *Do you want to be with one of them*, rambled and rattled and repeated itself.

Marle took the stairs two at a time, jogging to the door of room twenty-one. He knocked, and the door opened immediately.

"Why did you say that about me wanting to be with the men in the video?"

Rebecca shrugged. "It just seemed like the right thing to say. Do you want to come back in now?"

He sat on the edge of the bed and ground the heels of his hands against his eyeballs.

"It's okay, Marle." Rebecca sat down next to him. "You're certainly not the only one."

"But I don't even know if I am." He looked at her, letting his hands fall between his knees.

"Well," she said. "Is it always two guys and a girl?"

"Mostly."

"Why is that?"

"I don't even know why I'm talking to you about this."

"Say what you need to say, Marle."

"Why do I need to say anything?"

"I think you just need to admit something to yourself."

Marle sighed and felt his chest crumple like a kicked-in cardboard box. What was there to admit? Okay, yes, he thought: he'd long told himself that his eyes traced over bulgy male arms and legs out of jealousy, a twisty desire to transform his body from its pale scrawniness into the god-like thickness he watched on the screen. But he knew, even if he never let himself think it, that part of him wanted that, to touch it, feel its radiant warmth, know what coursed beneath all that perfect skin. Feel the curve of those lips and callused fingers.

"That's good, Marle."

"I didn't say anything."

"I can tell you're saying it in your own way."

Marle stood, shaking his head. "I need to get out of here."

"Okay, Marle."

"Okay?"

Rebecca shrugged.

Marle went to the window and flicked at the curtain with a finger. A quick glance told him the march of the frogs was continuing, growing, bulging out like a fast-acting tumor.

"What about them?"

"I told you, Marle. They're here to stink up the place. They're moving, but they have nowhere to go."

"And what about you?" He turned to her.

"What about me?"

"Do you have somewhere to go?"

"I think I'm where I'm meant to be."

"This has all been very strange."

She nodded. "Life's like that, I suppose."

Marle left. He didn't say goodbye.

He let the sound of the frogs wash over him, a shower of arrhythmic, syncopated noise. His blood pattered in time to the loudest croaks, and as he leaned against the walkway's guard rail, he watched the sun rise. Becky would arrive soon, treading a squishy path through the throng, tires squelching with the guts and blood and bones of frogs, and then, perhaps, he would cross the sea of ribbiting bodies, climb on his bike—he didn't own a car—and maneuver past them on the shoulder of the highway, rumble strip knocking his insides about, shedding his skin, turning him into someone new.

The Itch

Cree lifted her sandwich from the shallow Tupperware, one of the many that her mother religiously stacked in the cabinet above the stove's exhaust fan, then froze mid-bite. Brian Henderson had just walked into the Culver Community College student center dining room looking, as always, like a movie star as he approached a table full of baseball players and their girlfriends. He had shocked everyone fifteen months ago when he walked into their high school on the first day of senior year wearing a tie-dyed T-shirt that said, in bold, black, screen-printed letters: I LIKE BOYS. At lunch his friends had stared at him as he approached with a double cheeseburger perched on his tray, and Brian looked down at his chest. The room went silent as every clique, from the cheerleaders to the LARPers, stared. Brian shrugged and dropped one of his hands from his tray. He slugged Patrick Donahue, the starting catcher, on the shoulder, and said, "Move over so I can sit down, asshole."

Cree set the sandwich back in the Tupperware and scooted out of her chair, careful to walk in a long loop away from the baseball players, inconspicuous and unnoticed as she sidled up to the vending machines, where she splurged and bought a noisy bag of corn chips. She then scuttled back to her seat in the corner, glancing at Brian as she passed. He'd made some kind of joke and the rest of the red-faced kids at the table were laughing. One guy started choking on a chicken strip.

Cree looked down at the closed container. Making Cree sandwiches seemed to be her mother's idea of what it meant to be a good parent, because she'd been slathering mayonnaise and mustard onto marbled rye bread and stacking the slices with cold cuts and packaged cheese ever since Cree was in kindergarten. Never mind her mother's other failings: never telling Cree about menstruation and tampons, about birth control, about the dangers (or lack thereof) of drugs and beers. Forget that her mother never believed Cree when she accused some of her mother's revolving door of boyfriends of trying to cop a feel, even when her mother caught Carl, her most recent ex, peering into Cree's bedroom while she pretended to sleep. Every time they fought about anything— Cree wanting a job, wanting to go away to a four-year school instead of the community college, wanting clothing not purchased at Goodwill—her mother brought up the sandwiches, the sandwiches, the fucking sandwiches, as if putting together a bland meal for your only child somehow opened the door to parental sainthood and absolved you of all past wrongdoings. This was food, Cree thought, not the rosary. She couldn't wait to escape, even if she didn't know how that escape would come.

She couldn't say for sure, but she was pretty confident that she was the first to notice the scratching. Cree sat at the back of the biology lab, a hot, windowless room with eight workstations arranged in two rows. Cree's lab partner, a tall blonde girl with long fingers and a whisper for a voice, was absent, so she prepared her slides alone. Manda was nice, and actually pretty smart—she scored A's on all the tests in the lecture course—but something didn't compute when it came to the practical activities like dissection and microscopic observation. As a literature major, Manda was good at processing written information but seemed incapable of functioning without being a bumbling mess in the real world. Who, though, really could?

Brian Henderson, that's who, Cree thought, as Dr. Warren walked them through the final bit of slide preparation and overviewed the main steps in the lab, even though they were written in bold, bullet-pointed instructions on the worksheet. Cree only half-listened, focusing on the kids in front of her, who were all beginning to reach their hands toward their scalps. Brian Henderson sat in the very front row, on the far left nearest the door. She watched the muscles in his forearms twitch as he dug into his hair, fingers pinching at a swirling cowlick.

Dr. Warren paused, blinking. She surveyed the class like a roving camera. "Is everyone okay?" she said. Cree felt fine. Her hair was soft, her scalp free of itchy tingles. She watched bitten nails and painted nails, hands covered in veins, hair, eczema, reaching up toward frizzed hair, curled hair, buzzcuts. Wide-eyed, Dr. Warren blinked behind her glasses and then, as if making a horrific discovery in a disaster movie, raised her own hand up to the crown of her head, digging her nails—plain, well-manicured—into the part in her own hair.

Her mother was out when Cree arrived at the house, a tiny bungalow squeezed into a dusty, weedy neighborhood of dilapidated ranches. The nearest grocery store was a Piggly Wiggly, and all the surrounding restaurants were scuzzy bars filled with cigar smoke, not that Cree would be stepping into any of those—legally, at least—for another two years. The two-bedroom house she shared with her mother smelled like artificial lemon spray, because her mother emptied aerosol bottles in droves to usher away the odor of the clove cigarettes she vacuumed into her lungs in front of the television, clouds of smoke collecting near the ceiling and turning the walls a dull yellow. Her mother told Cree she'd kill her if she took up the habit herself, and Cree winced and shook her head, not bothering to tell her that she had no intentions of ever doing such a thing. She had no plans on ever doing anything the way her mother did.

Cree dropped her bag next to her desk and fell onto her bed. When she was younger, she'd been obsessed with outer space, so her ceiling was dotted with glow-in-the-dark plastic stars that pulsed a neon green in the dark. She didn't have the energy to pluck them down, so every night her room lit up like a planetarium, and sometimes Cree would shut one eye so the room spun just so. She imagined herself tilting through outer space, weightless, the milky marble of Earth falling away behind her.

By the time her mother came home, Cree had planted herself on the living room sofa and was watching the news. The lead story was about the sudden infestation of lice rampaging through local schools, not only plaguing the hygiene-inept kindergarteners but the teachers and staff as well. And reports were coming in that grocery stores and office buildings had been hit by the spaz of bugs, too, businesses shutting down all across the county. Cree's mother blustered in, carrying a cloud of smoke from her half-chuffed cigarette.

"Gross shit!" her mother yelled, startling Cree. She waved toward the television. "We had to shut down early because of that." On weekdays she worked the lunch shift at Brick's, a shitty bar and grill that burned their burgers and sent out the fries either cold or too crispy. Every dish was served with a side of ranch dressing, but there were no salads on the menu. Sometimes, like today, Cree's mother stuck around through the early ramp of the dinner rush, when the alcoholics and cheaters stopped in for a Crown and Coke or a pair of Brick's signature Low-Class Mimosas (half a bullet of champagne, a splash of Sunny D, and a shot of Popov vodka) that were two for one during happy hour.

Cree's mother knew all the regular clientele and they tipped well, especially when, like now, she wore one of her low-cut tops. She reached into her purse, shiny faux leather with a pair of obviously fake golden G's hot-glued to the strap, and extracted a few clumps of damp bills, dropping them on the coffee table. Cree unfolded the bills, arranging them in denominational order. Her mother never counted her earnings at Brick's, convinced one of the sleazy busboys would try to skim her take if she set up at one of the high tops after her shift was over and started advertising her tips like the other waitresses did. Cree was pretty sure her mother couldn't actually count, or was, at the very least, too lazy to figure out their finances. The benefit to Cree was that she could easily take a small divot out of her mother's earnings, slipping out a five or a few singles once her mom had turned away.

Cree pulled her legs out from under her and shuffled toward the kitchen. The tile was old, the grout dissolved between the gray terra cotta that was, more than not, spattered with bits of hardened food, wizened sawdust of rye bread, and globs of coagulated mayo and Grey Poupon. She watched her mother wave her hand in front of her face as if she'd gotten a whiff of something dying. She bounced on her heels with more physical effort than Cree could ever remember her mother exhibiting. "What?" Cree said. Her mother turned, eyes welling with tears that were smearing up her already-uneven mascara. She waved her hands, her hot-pink painted nails pointed in the direction of her scalp.

"I itch! It itches!"

Cree backed away.

"What do I do?" Her mother hopped from one foot to the other, refusing to rake her hands through her hair. Credit where it was due, Cree thought to herself: Her mother had just been to the salon bright and early that morning, and no matter how many bugs were scampering through her locks now, she wouldn't upset the new 'do.

Classes were canceled the next two days. Not officially, but every one of Cree's professors sent a class-wide email insisting that students stay home and visit a pharmacy to pick up lice-killing shampoo.

"Spend some time contemplating the rise and fall of Rome while you lather and kill those suckers," her history instructor wrote. He was skinny and near-sighted but didn't wear glasses, so if you didn't sit in the front row, he had no idea who you were. Cree, still infestation-free, sat in front of the television, keeping away from her mother and Andrew, the newest conquest. Brick's was closed for two days, too, so Cree had to turn up the volume on the TV when her mother and Andrew slid into the bedroom for their afternoon hump sessions. Andrew was maybe three or four years Cree's senior, and ruddy like wet clay. He had the body of a former football player, chunked with size but lacking tone, unworked muscles gone to fat.

The message board in Cree's bio lab was active because a test was coming up in less than a week. Dr. Warren had offered only to move it back one class period because their review session was nuked by the lice outbreak. Some members of the class, led by Manda, were planning a meet-up once the bugs were gone, and anyone who wished to cram for the test was welcome to meet on Saturday in the campus library, second floor, one p.m. Manda had already reserved one of the group work carrels. Cree saw that Brian Henderson had posted that he'd be there—he needed help remembering the process of cell diffusion, in particular—so Cree RSVP'd in the positive, too, eliciting a thumbs up emoji from Brian only a few minutes later. She felt herself flush.

By Saturday, her mother had finally returned to Brick's, piling on two double shifts in a row to make up for lost cash. Andrew was sprawled out in her mother's bed like a squatter, the door cracked so Cree could see his naked torso and hairy feet, and she felt, for the first time, the itchy shiver that had plagued everyone else for the past few days. But instead of crawling through her scalp, the tiny dots of scratchiness bit at her arms and legs and back. She shivered and tossed herself out the door, realizing, as she settled into the old Buick her mother had bought for a grand a year ago, that she was heading to school without one of her mother's sandwiches for the first time she could remember.

The library smelled like cheap carpet cleaner and the odor intensified in the study carrel where six students were clustered, textbooks yawning open on the table before them. The seat across from Brian Henderson was unoccupied, but when Cree sat down, the lawless giddiness that had sprung up in her dissipated: Brian's left hand was splayed atop that of the boy sitting next to him, and Cree had to watch their lovey-dovey antics up close, including the twitches of their bodies as they played a poorly hidden game of footsy. Brian glanced across the table at Cree from time to time, a mysterious look on his face, as if he were working on some complicated math problem. Every time, Cree looked away.

The room, with its one high window pouring in afternoon sunlight, grew hot fast. Cree felt her T-shirt dampen under her breasts and at her lower back, and she shifted with an itchy discomfort where her legs chafed against her chair's upholstery. Manda led the charge through mitosis, passing around handouts she'd made for everyone, her loopy handwriting cramping and smushing as it darted across the pages. Cree knew all of this already. She glanced at her phone, watching the time tick away.

Two hours in, Brian laughed at something his boyfriend—Davey, as he'd been introduced—said, which seemed to break the spell of monotony. Another student, a girl who smelled like Fritos and wore a smock dress that must have increased her body temperature past boiling, yawned, shut her book, and said she was tapped out. They talked then about the lice, spraying out uncomfortable laughter at their dismay that such a childhood infestation had managed to gouge into each of them now that they were springy, vibrant adults. Cree kept her mouth shut, feigning her own awkward chortles, and nodding in agreement when Kellyanne Porter, a squat, bespectacled girl, recounted how her mother had raged at the college's ineptitude when it came to allowing such an outbreak. "She blames the Childhood Development building," Kellyanne said, shoving at the bridge of her glasses, which had slid down her nose.

Before they left, Brian announced that he and his roommates were throwing a party the next Saturday at the Valley View Apartments near campus. He gave the building number to everyone. "You should all come. For real," he said, his gaze lingering on Cree, or so she thought. "After this monster test, we could all use a beer, you know?"

Cree blinked and nodded as she stuffed her textbook into her bag. She rushed out into the air-conditioned chill of the library stacks, body tingling at the cold. She'd been to only one party, a kegger at some doofus jock's house a few weekends before all of the kids who'd managed to get admitted to out-of-state schools jetted off to Miami and New York and Utah. Cree had spent the night nursing a single strawberry wine cooler, the gritty, syrupy liquid too sweet for her. She'd mostly stood in the corner of the back porch, looking around for Brian. When he did arrive, orchestrating various drinking games and seeming to win all of them, she watched but didn't approach him. He was surrounded by a glom of former cheerleaders and other baseball players, and flirted with wanton abandon with everyone within reach, once slapping Patrick Donahue on the ass.

Cree went to his party a week later. No one had talked about the lice that week, as if a gag order had been put in place. Her classmates periodically reached up absently to gouge at the parts in their hair, dig under headbands, adjust bobby pins or baseball caps. Her mother made her more sandwiches. Cree didn't really need to sneak out Saturday night; her mother was working a closing shift, wouldn't be home, carrying the smell of cigars and Cabo Wabo on her clothes, until after two a.m. Cree could get back in plenty of time.

She knew the Valley View Apartments: industrial-style lofts built across the street from campus. Brian's building wasn't the frontmost, where a bookstore and a hookah bar took up half the first-floor commercial units. She snaked her car down a steep hill to a small lot in the back, where two other buildings, with traditional two-bedroom apartments on the first floor and lofts stacked above, sat. Brian's building was on the left, the apartment on the corner of the second floor. Cree could already see bodies squished onto the tiny iron-ringed balcony. Most of the parking spaces were filled with cars plastered with college decals, so she had to park even farther away, around the back of the building in an even smaller lot, where the only empty spots were near a smelly dumpster that wafted out the smell of rotting fruit. Cree ambled around the building to the elevator, punching in the code Brian had given at the library. The sounds of the party were muffled but audible in the wide, carpeted hallway that reminded her of a high-rise hotel, and the noise grew as she approached the door. She considered knocking, but then shook her head at her own foolishness and simply turned the knob and stepped inside. The loft was two-storied, a huge living room, dining room, and kitchen combo on the first floor, an iron spiral staircase leading up to the second. An orange Gatorade cooler was perched on the granite countertop separating the kitchen and its stainless-steel appliances from the living room. The apartment was tropically warm; bodies spread their musky smells of cologne and perfume and off-brand deodorant into a sticky miasma of artificial flowers and sweat.

There were at least thirty people on the main floor, some of whom Cree vaguely recognized but couldn't name, a half-dozen of them sitting at a pub-height dining room table, playing cards. She pulled a plastic cup from a sleeve by the cooler, filled it with cherry-red liquid, and stood watching as a muscular, tan boy with a crew cut shuffled the cards. He glanced up at Cree, and she took a sip from her drink (too sweet, definitely boozy, the sharp tang of Everclear making her tongue curl). She shook her head when he asked if she wanted to be dealt in. No one else at the table looked at her as they started gathering the cards he slid across to them.

Cree watched as the players laid down cards and pointed at one another, doling out drinks. One girl howled in gleeful rage when the dealer assigned her a dozen slurps from her cup. When she'd drained the whole thing, she let out a ululation, her tongue cartoonishly red from the punchy liquid.

Cree scanned the room. A television in the living area was set to a music station blasting classic rock from the 1980s. People were packed on the two couches that made up the living room seating, brown microfiber things. The girls were in cutoffs or loose, billowy dresses, the guys in khaki shorts and T-shirts. Cree, in a smart white blouse and soft green capris, felt out of place. She could hear the squad on the couch talking about the lice, how one grade school was still dealing with the infestation, a word that made two of the girls seated together squeal with disgust.

No one from the study group was on the ground floor, so she decided to climb the spiral staircase. As she made her way up, she marveled that anyone her age, at her school, could afford such a place. The lighting was soft, the acoustics generous. Exposed duct work slithered along the vaulted ceiling. From above, the granite of the kitchen sparkled like something in *Better Homes and Gardens*. She imagined Brian Henderson serving champagne and strawberries to guests, talking about a recent polo match or a cruise on his forty-foot yacht.

Cree felt an itch in her scalp as she reached the second floor. She took a deep swig from her cup. From below, the sounds of the party swirled up toward her, a mash of voices and thumping music.

Two second-floor doors were cracked open, wide enough that Cree could see they were bedrooms, both dark, the flooring the same hard bluish-gray cement as on the ground floor. The nearer room was tiny, barely enough space for a queen-size bed and a dresser. She slipped inside and sat on the end of the bed. Her head was pulsing.

Cree felt the itch again and she plucked at her scalp. Something wriggled and she crushed it between her fingers. Nausea crept up her throat, a buzzy heat, and she wiped the dead bug off on the bedspread. She knew she had to leave, get out of the party before someone discovered that she'd become infected on some kind of gruesomely unkind time delay. But Cree was fastened to the bed, the muscles of her legs overwhelmed by a strange fatigue. The room spun, tilting like a rocking boat.

The bedroom door swung open, the noise from downstairs barging in. Cree's eyes widened, and she saw Brian Henderson and his boyfriend standing there, arms slung over one another.

"Oh," Brian said, voice piquant with sudsy beer. "Hey."

"Sorry," Cree said. "I just needed someplace quiet."

"No worries," he said, untangling himself from Davey, who stood grinning like a weasel, hand drizzling across Brian's back as they separated. Brian gestured, twisting his body from Davey toward Cree. "This is the girl."

The girl. The way Brian said it, the way Davey stared—one eyebrow raised, a smile trying to gurgle its way into his lips—made a queasy warmth lap over Cree, temporarily stomping down the itchiness now ramping up its intensity in her scalp.

"The girl," Davey said. "You didn't say so last week at the library."

For the first time Cree could remember, Brian looked embarrassed. "It didn't seem appropriate at the time."

Davey gaped. "You? Worried about appropriate?"

Brian gave Davey's chest a smack.

Cree had no idea what was happening, and although she could feel her jaw slacking, her mouth open in movie-trope confusion, she couldn't move, because if she did, she'd start scratching at her scalp again.

"She's confused," Davey said. "Maybe you should explain."

Brian let out a teapot breath. "Okay. This won't be embarrassing at all."

"Just tell her. What's the worst that could happen?"

Cree managed to bring her cup to her lips, only to discover it was empty. She pretended to drink.

"I had a huge crush on you in high school," Brian blurted.

More warmth washed over Cree, swirling with the alcohol darting through her bloodstream. She felt like she was glowing.

"You did?" she said, her mouth feeling chewy. Her head was a wriggling hive, and she almost patted at her hair, certain Davey and Brian could see the lice drilling around her scalp. "But you're—you know."

"Oh." Brian blinked. Davey let out a sorry chuckle, and Cree knew she'd said something wrong.

"Aren't you? You wore that shirt."

Brian shook his head. "That damn shirt. I should have taken a marker to it and written *And Girls* at the end."

"You like both?"

"Sure do. I'm a switch hitter."

"I thought you were a pitcher," Cree said.

Davey let out a roar. "I'm sorry," he said. "This is too funny."

Cree's gaze moved from the one boy to the other. "What's funny? What is it?"

"Nothing," Brian said, glaring at Davey. He moved into the room and sat down next to Cree. "Don't worry about it."

"I said something wrong." Cree cringed. She felt like she was watching a movie of herself. She was floating above and beyond, judging and staring and hating what she saw but unable to stop it.

Brian patted her arm. "You're not the first. You won't be the last."

A weight settled into Cree's chest, cracking against her ribs, pressing toward her heart. She found breathing suddenly difficult with Brian Henderson's fingers brushing against the soft pliancy of her upper arm. His hand was warm, electric, and she felt a jolt in her middle that vanished when he let go.

"I think I need to pee," she said, standing. "I'm sorry I barged into your bedroom."

Brian stood. "It's okay. Really. We all need quiet time, you know?"

Cree nodded and shoved past Davey, who was still smiling, cocksure and obnoxious, his face a blotchy blur as she left the room. She imagined how he would laugh at her expense right before he kissed Brian, climbed atop his body and used it, abused it, shook it, shuddered with the delight of it. Her brain pulsed with images of the two of them piled onto one another, bodies interlocked like puzzle pieces, teeth rattling against skin, biting and grating. She tried to shake the image as she swirled down the spiral staircase, the noise of the party ricocheting in her head, the itch at her scalp intensifying. She felt like she was being punctured all over, a crown of needles spiking into her skin.

She found a washroom with a sink and toilet and a wicker trash can with a white liner. Cree tossed her empty cup in it, where it joined a used condom and some balled-up Kleenex. She sat on the closed toilet lid and ground the heels of her palms against her eyes. Brian's voice thundered in her head, milky and soft. She swam through her memories of high school, already feeling dim and long-ago. She had spent so many lunch hours taking furtive glances toward the boisterous table of baseball players, his hawking laugh and sure voice the loudest, telling raunchy jokes and slinging pedantic insults at the outfielders. Surely he'd been lying about his crush, some kind of off-the-cuff kindness to get her out of the bedroom so he and Davey could hook up, do whatever slick, sweaty things they planned to do to one another.

Someone knocked on the bathroom door. Cree croaked out a "Just a minute," stood up, and splashed some water on her face. She gritted her teeth—the lice were thick like a shower cap—and flung open the door. A girl, mascara running tracks down her cheeks, blew by her, howling. She lurched over to the toilet and barely had time to fling the seat up before she was horking a technicolor wave of vomit into the bowl, one hand on the side of the porcelain, the other clawing at her hair.

The girl took a breath and looked back at Cree, her body humping with exertion. "It's happening again! Why?"

Cree looked out at the party. What had been a relaxed gathering was transforming into an edgy mess. Boys were scratching at their scalps while girls tittered and shouted. At least half of the partygoers were stomping out the door.

"Why, why, why, why?" the girl kneeling before the toilet intoned, as if speaking in tongues or casting a spell over the white Kohler bowl. She looked up at Cree, who blinked. "This was supposed to be over."

Cree looked from the party to the girl, then twisted around to look at herself in the mirror. She tried to see whatever Brian Henderson saw, whatever it was her mother never seemed to see, what it was Cree wanted to see. Everything was blurry at the edges, jittery and uncertain. She ran her fingers along the top of her head. The lice were in there, she knew, burrowing and making a home.

"I'm not sure," Cree said, "that this kind of thing can ever really be over." She and the girl locked eyes while she dug into her scalp, letting her fingernails cut into her own skin. "The more you scratch," she said, "the worse things get."

Flytrap

When the bugs started coalescing on the windshield, Bennett thought it just another part of a hot Missouri summer night. He'd been bombarded by wolfish mosquitos, pestered by bippy-bopping gnats, and listened to the churn of cicadas and crickets for years. He'd chased after lightning bugs as a kid, setting a jar full of them loose in his house while his mother screeched and hid in the kitchen, waiting until they were dead to sweep them out from behind the sofa like fallen, defunct Christmas lights. So when a cluster of flies the size of a catcher's mitt landed on the windshield and blocked Humphrey Bogart's face in the middle of *Casablanca* showing on the big screen, he thought nothing of it.

The date had been Matthew's idea. He admitted to Bennett, with no shame whatsoever, that he loved movies and rued the Grand's closure four years ago after a tornado ripped apart the concession stand and tore a hole the size of a shed through the big screen; when the theatre had announced it was reopening, he'd circled the opening weekend on his calendar, set an alarm on his phone. But Matthew was currently without vehicle following a gnarly accident in which he'd been t-boned by a drunk driver, and his car was totaled. He had shitty insurance that wouldn't cover a rental, he told Bennett, and he'd just started at his job working IT support from home for one of those online auction sites that promise you can buy a new Macbook for fifty-three ninety-nine, so they had to take Bennett's clunker, which might as well have been totaled itself. The AC was on the fritz, the radio fuzzed in and out, and the passenger side hand-crank window didn't like to roll all the way up.

They both managed the sweaty tinge on their necks by chugging bottled water and shushing their angry bladders, but the window posed a problem when the one clot of flies became two and then three and then suddenly they were flitting in through the window, which refused to budge no matter how much Matthew grunted at the hand-crank.

They swarmed the popcorn Matthew had bought at the concession stand, handfuls of which had left his lips glossy with butter that Bennett had hoped to eventually kiss onto his own mouth, inhaling the salty warmth of Matthew's breath. They flitted into the open box of Junior Mints Matthew had brought along. He'd frozen them that morning so that when he popped one into Bennett's mouth it sat on his tongue like a pebble washed smooth in a mountain stream. The flies covered the straws on their sweating paper cups of soda they'd spiked with spiced rum. They tittered over the gear shift, the steering wheel, the dashboard. When Bennett fluttered his hands toward them, they buzzed into a cyclone of proboscises and wings, exoskeletons and compound eyes, and resettled somewhere else.

Bennett glanced out his window. Between the black holes of flies on the glass he could see that other cars were being bombarded. A woman who had snuck out of her vehicle for a restroom break was shrieking, windmilling her hands around her head, hair tangled with flies. She appeared to be spitting to keep them from her lips. A cluster was gathered on her ankle like a moving, smeary tattoo. When Bennett flicked the windshield wipers on, the flies tornadoed up, some of them trapped by the squealing rubber knives, their bodies bursting, dragged along the glass. More flies resettled in their place, tiny pincer legs wheedling at the guts of their fallen brethren.

Matthew started slapping at the glove box, the door handle, the window with the back of his hand, caking his knuckles in fly innards. He peeled off his shirt and pressed it to the cracked window to prevent more of them from seeping in, but they found their way around the fabric, which couldn't clog the entire gap.

"This is insane," he said. "This is not normal."

Bennett agreed, willing himself not to linger on Matthew's hip bones. He reached back behind his seat and found his gym bag. From inside he plucked out a ratty towel in need of a wash; if it weren't for the fly infestation, he'd be worried about the funk fuming off it, something yellow and fleshy. But he figured a little human stink was better than drowning in fly guts and wings, so he stifled his embarrassment and handed the crinkled towel over to Matthew, who shoved it toward the window, pushing the fabric through with his fingertips. Flies banged around, landing and feeling out the threads, drawn to the dried sweat crusted into the weave. At least Matthew would know that Bennett worked out, which had to be appealing.

"Should we get out of here?" Matthew said.

Bennett craned his neck to see through a blank spot in the windshield that was growing ever more crowded. He tried spritzing it with some washer fluid, which sent the flies into a tizzy but also created a swampy muck across the glass. He turned up the wipers' speed, and they chunk-thunked across the windshield. Now the swamp was a tarry mass like gloopy asphalt.

"I think they've descended upon the screen," Bennett said, ducking his head so he could see through one tiny bit of clear windowpane. "Ingrid Bergman looks like she has some seriously problematic blackheads."

"Ugh. What a nightmare."

"Clearasil is not fixing that."

Matthew smiled, but then a trio of flies dive-bombed his teeth. He sputtered and wrenched his open palm toward his face.

Bennett started killing more flies, ignoring the growing slop of insect guts glooped to his knuckles. He whacked at his seatback, at the dashboard, at the driver side window. Soon Matthew joined him, clubbing the glove compartment with the Junior Mint box.

"Nice one," Bennett said when Matthew took down an entire swath of them. The bugs cluttered to the floor, drizzling the mats and sliding along the brake and gas pedals. It became a game, who could kill more. They slapped at their own bodies, leaving greenish-yellow smears along their thighs and stomachs. Dead flies swirled into their arm hair and along the rippled space between Matthew's pecs.

The movie had long stopped playing. Outside the car, they could hear screeching tires as moviegoers tried to escape. Voices carried through the heavy buzz of wings and sawing exoskeletons. Neither of them could see out of the car anymore; every window was covered in a mass of flies. The interior had gone dark, and so Bennett reached up through the thrum and poked at the manual overhead light. In the gloom, they looked like warriors from a bloody battle.

More dead flies than live were left in the car. The air was sour with sweat and the oozy aura of so many crushed bugs. Their bodies glistened with effort and insect carrion. Bennett pulled off his shirt and turned it inside out. He started wiping himself off, pausing periodically to lunge at a fly brave enough to move.

"Here," he said, reaching into his gym bag and finding a pair of running shorts. "You can clean yourself up."

Matthew took the shorts and used the hem to wipe his face; he'd slapped himself silly trying to kill the flies aiming at his nostrils, and blackish streaks poured across his cheekbones like runny mascara.

"Helluva date," he said when he tossed the gored shorts into the back seat.

"One for the record books," Bennett said. "Tell the grandkids one day."

They looked at one another, the only noise the dizzy cavorting of a fly bopping along the ceiling, feeling at the smashed bodies of its brethren.

"I didn't mean—" Bennett started.

"Shh," Matthew said. "It's okay."

He reached out a stained finger and pressed it to Bennett's lips, then leaned in and kissed him. They both tasted like rancid, fetid flies, but neither backed away or grimaced. They pressed their tongues through lips, against teeth. Brought their hands to each other's naked shoulders. They let themselves transcend, fly away from the moment and the buzzing and, for the moment, into the wild, unknowable future.

Back Swing

When their father Paul announced he was going to spend his inheritance building a miniature golf course on the family land, Troy Buckingham and his sisters experienced a collective premonition of disaster. Troy saw his college fund smoking in a barren, heaping pile, smelling of dung and rancid milk. He pictured himself working at a gas station and living in his basement bedroom until he was forty. He would never lose his virginity, not with Heather Beilman or Saul Fleischman, who took turns inhabiting his dreams, each one leaving him dry-mouthed and achy. His sisters groaned over their father's blandishments about the windmill, the gopher mound at the fourteenth hole, the on-site creamery where a cadre of cows would produce milk they would churn into ice cream and sell by the cone. Elodie, the eldest daughter, lamented the end of her expensive private cello lessons; Maggie felt the evaporation of her dreams of owning a pony; Caroline, who wanted to be an artist ever since her trip to the St. Louis Art Museum, knew she would never have her own easels and expensive paints.

"We'll call the place *Hole-y Cow*," their father said.

Elodie groaned. Maggie and Caroline laughed. Troy bit into his black bean burger. He could feel his father's eyes on him, pulsing him with a pleading look. Troy's father regularly burdened him with these heavy glances, as if the fact that they were the only two with Y chromosomes in the house meant they had to forge some kind of alliance. But Troy thought the idea of a miniature golf course and ice cream shoppe (his father *insisted* the old-style spelling would increase the charm of the place and thus foot traffic) was as stupid as stupid could get.

Their house sat on a huge swath of land that neither their father, their father's father, nor his father had been willing to sell, even when commercial developers salivated over it, offering well over market value. The land was located off interstate 70, close to other land developments where apartment complexes, a Toyota dealership, even a Home Depot and a sprawling subdivision filled with identical Spanish villas had sprung up in the last dozen years. Fifteen acres spilled back in golden waves, used for grazing cattle ("We already have the milking operation half-running!" their father said, slapping his hand on the dining room table). They would be able to live where they worked, so no commute, no fighting traffic, and no exorbitant gas expenditures at the QT down the road.

So the kids said fine, fine. Troy looked at his sisters. What else could they do but wrinkle their lips in hopeless surrender while their father went on about what color golf balls he would order?

"Now," he said. "What do you all think of a magic-themed course?"

It took a year to construct the golf course. His father filed permits, bought a mattress system, a feeding fence, buckets of stall cleaner. He let Elodie design the ice cream shoppe, choose the dipper wells, the commercial freezers, the melamine pans and scoopers. Troy watched her click through various online stores, talking to herself about whether they should make their own waffle cones or buy them pre-shaped. Troy marveled at his sister's savvy, how, at the prospect of becoming a *store manager*, her otherwise artsy-fartsy musical side melted away like so much ice. Her cello sat forgotten.

Maggie and Caroline exhorted their father to fill the course with castles, castles, castles! And as many vibrant colors of ice cream as possible! They didn't care about pasteurizers or cheese vats, chart recorders or milk pumps. They dreamt of hitting vibrant pink and purple golf balls through the mouths of burpy toads, the craggy legs of ogres, around marshy moats surrounding fairy book towers. They offered up their own hole designs, complete with monstrous waterfalls, greens that spiraled three stories high, and a dragon that shot out real flames if you sunk a hole in one. Their father compromised by purchasing a plastic monstrosity with wings the size of a small sedan. Its eyes showered the seventh hole with infernal red light after dusk.

At first, they served only the basics: chocolate and vanilla ice cream. Then their father caught some creativity bug and started branching out: cherry and pineapple, caramel, cookies 'n' cream. Then wilder flavors. People adored the pistachio, which Troy scooped it out in green mound after green mound. There was a charcoal concoction that the hipsters swooned over, and when they unveiled the newest mystery flavor, people crowed over the champagne ice cream, available only to adults over twenty-one. Some of the kids home from college for summer vacations gawked when Troy carded them. He would shrug and offer a sheepish smile, and when he could tell an ID was fake, he sold the ice cream anyway. He was pretty sure no one was going to get drunk off his father's spumante-tinged treats, and since when did Alcohol, Tobacco, and Firearms plot sting operations on miniature golf courses?

His classmates came in foursomes; some of the jocks were drunk or stoned or both, but Troy's father didn't have a substance-free policy, so Troy handed over the rubber-and-steel putters without a word. College kids wearing too-large glasses and an excess of scarves showed up, the girls giggling about their terrible aim, the boys feigning disinterest in getting the lowest score but pumping their fists when they shot under par. Customers' tan arms and legs slicked with sweat even in late evening. They ignored the sweet and sour loam smell of cow dung, calling it part of the experience, all for the sake of down home, local ice cream. Rich, buttered, creamy, organic, and supporting a local business. The strawberry, with real, chunky fruit swirled in, was to die for.

Troy watched his classmates laugh their way through eighteen holes then plop down together on metal tables strewn near the concession stand. Patio umbrellas sponsored by Michelob Ultra fluttered in the windy nights while kids crammed themselves onto the circular bench seats, boys slipping their palms against girls' thighs. Girlfriends leaned into boyfriends, whispering sweet nothings into perking ears. Cheeks were pecked, lips were locked. Troy's heart broke when Heather Beilman and Saul Fleischman showed up on a date, hands slipping into one another's back pockets as they left. Three little league baseball teams came one night, and Troy's arms were sore in the morning from moving around tins of ice cream when Elodie needed help restocking.

But his father was raking in the dough. No worries about Troy's college fund. Elodie could keep her lessons, though now she wanted to go into restaurant management and interior design, erstwhile dreams of Juilliard and a place in the Boston Symphony Orchestra abandoned. Maggie still didn't have a pony, but Caroline had started smearing paints on her first easel.

All was well in the Buckingham household until the day the first cow died.

Troy and his sisters didn't interact with the livestock except for when they got in trouble, such as after the night Troy snuck out with his best friend Clay Ridgemore and got drunk off a bottle of Johnnie Walker and came home so hungover the next morning that he vomited in the bathroom near the ninth hole three times. His father made him spend the next day sweeping out the milking barn just because; there was no reason to swish away the clods of dirt, cow turd, and mulchy grass, because every time the cattle were corralled for a milking the concrete floor was stained again. After the one time Elodie had been put through it for her own elopement to a mall and then a party where, she claimed, she very much did *not* drink the spiked punch, but stayed out until well after her curfew, she raised such hell, screaming that she would call child services and the health department and the Better Business Bureau if she was made to do that ever again, their father promised never to make her go near the cows again.

So it was Tim, the farmhand they'd hired, a stringy-haired kid from Nebraska with a deep voice and a wicked farmer's tan who was looking to forge out on his own rather than spend his whole life in corn fields forty minutes outside of Omaha, who came huffing up to the course the morning everything went to hell. Sometimes Troy had to stop from staring at the columns of wiry muscle in his back when he worked shirtless.

"Something's wrong with Moo," he said to Troy, huffing. Tim was lithe and lean, but apparently his cardiovascular system could use an overhaul. "Where's your dad?"

Troy pointed toward the office in the back of the concession stand where his father kept a computer on which he worked spreadsheets to track business expenditures and intakes. The room, small and crowded with candy bar wrappers and crinkly, empty bags of chips, smelled of the air freshener pumping out the artificial aroma of apples and cinnamon. Troy listened from the cashier window while Tim whispered. Troy's father shot out of his squeaky desk chair like a missile and charged out of the concession stand, Tim in fast pursuit. Blinking, Troy made an executive decision, pulling the displayed putters and golf balls from the counter and yanking down the corrugated metal window guard. He followed his father.

Paul Buckingham had thought he'd been doing a nice thing in letting each of his kids name one of the milking cows. Troy had still been dumpy and disbelieving, so when his father pointed to the large bovine body that his eldest son would christen, Troy, arms folded over his chest and a dead-eyed look on his face, declared that his cow would be named Moo.

And by the time Troy, his father, and Tim reached the barn, Moo was mooing no more.

Paul Buckingham called a vet, who couldn't figure it out. No signs of anaplasmosis or blue green algae toxicity. No prussic acid. There was no evidence of perilla mint on the grounds. The vet, a barrel-shaped man with a beard beaded with sweat and streaked gray, plucked off his latex gloves with a puff of talcum powder, wiped his hands on his jeans, and then shrugged at Troy's father. He couldn't explain Moo's death, advising only that they needed to call a licensed disposer to remove the body.

"It could infect the rest of them. The decomposing flesh, and whatever caused the death," he said.

Paul Buckingham made the call. A truck came out that afternoon. Men in space-age jumpsuits that glimmered white against the grass snapped on elbow-length gloves and hauled the cow away.

But even so, the others followed quickly, like dominos falling in a line. Cashmere (named by Elodie), Cuckoo (Maggie), Snarfle (Caroline). All dead, all fast.

"Mad cow?" their father said on the phone.

Not mad cow. None of the cattle suffered incoordination, trouble rising or walking. They'd all been their same complacent, lowing selves, tails swishing, udders dangling, heavy sacs. And then—thunk—they were dead. They'd have seen the signs of bovine spongiform encephalopathy well before Moo or Snarfle or any of the other cows croaked.

The remaining milking cows—five—seemed fine for a few days, but then two of them dropped on a Saturday morning.

Troy watched his father slumped in the office making frantic phone calls. He would slam the door shut, shaking the walls of the concession stand. His voice burbled like he was under water. Troy imagined him thrashing, thumping his fist on the rickety desk.

And then the other three cows pitched over Sunday morning. Tim delivered the news, his brow glistening with nerves. Troy was sure he'd been crying, which made him want to wrap his arms around Tim's wiry frame. With a good scrub, and maybe a haircut, Tim would be dashing, with his shelf of cheekbones and steel-blue eyes that were, at the moment, shot with blood. The dead cows were splayed on their sides in the meadow near the barn, open mouths seeping half-chewed cud. Their bodies were already bloated, the noxious smell of methane farting into the sky, the barn concentrated with it.

Elodie looked around, shifty-eyed, when customers asked why the ice cream supplies were so low. They kept serving what they had already churned; the vet didn't say to stop, their father argued. So let's make every scoop count. Who knows when we'll have more. So they scraped the bottom of the frozen serving tins, pulling every bit of ice cream they could. Before the cows started dying they'd skimmed and pasteurized several gallons yet to be churned, so there was still something.

The vanilla and chocolate ice cream ran out first. Customers gawked and wondered how an ice cream shoppe—a *shoppe*—ran out of vanilla.

"It's like a Taco Bell not having beef."

"Or chicken."

"Or tortillas."

"Um," Troy said, holding an empty cone in its white sleeve.

Their father stayed in the office well after the golf course was closed, the pathway lights blinkered off. Troy tried to think of things to say as he tidied up, slotting the putters in their cubbies and letting the balls clatter on their drying racks, sparkling and smooth after a wash in a bucket of hot tap water and dish soap. His jaw hinged open and shut as he wiped down the counter and then scrubbed at the sneeze guard over the ice cream, but nothing came out of his mouth. He felt like a balloon with a slow leak.

They bought two new milking cows after paying to have the entire barn sanitized from rafters to floor, the walls scrubbed clean with an antibacterial spray so strong none of them could enter for two days afterward.

Tim found those cows a week later, flies buzzing against their open, unblinking eyelids.

His sisters whispered about the cows, Caroline crying herself to sleep over the death of Snarfle. She announced at breakfast on Tuesday that she had prayed to God to bring the cows back to life, that she would never eat another scoop of ice cream her entire life if they would just be okay.

"You don't have to do that," Elodie said.

Troy was tired, ragged from a too-bright dream of Tim, who appeared suddenly in his bedroom, stripped of his shirt, muscles pulsing with size like he'd spent the last thirty minutes flexing. They had started kissing, Tim's hands raking through Troy's hair, fingers webbing around his ears and throat, pressing against his back and hips. He'd been awakened by the bubbling noises of his sisters talking, Maggie shrieking something about a stolen hairbrush, their voices vibrating along the shabby walls of the farmhouse's damp second floor.

He worked his jaw, which felt gummed up like a poorly-oiled piston.

"Tell her," Elodie said.

Troy sighed. "You don't need to pray over the cows."

"Yes I do!" Caroline said, nearly wailing. "How else will we get Snarfle back?"

Troy arched an eyebrow at Elodie. Their younger sisters had been strangely calm when their mother got sick three years ago, her cords of auburn hair replaced by vibrant bandanas, makeup sluiced off, pouches of exhaustion knitted beneath her eyes. Her cheeks went hollow instead of rouged. At her funeral, the girls cried, burbling out baby noises, but they never asked where their mother had gone or if she'd be back. The next morning, Troy and Elodie had found Maggie scrambling eggs, just like their mother had done the entirety of Maggie's nine-year-old life. Caroline was trying to pour orange juice, her little hands slipping against the carton. Troy had plucked it from her right before disaster struck. Seeing the fragile look on her face, he exhorted her to let him help, insisting she was the one guiding the orange fountain of juice down into each of the five glasses she'd managed to pull from their position in a cabinet.

They had approached death, Troy thought, with an unsettling aplomb, far less tormented than he was. Troy had been branded by tortuous nightmares of his mother, trapped inside a coffin and helplessly banging on the box's sides until her oxygen ran out or, somehow more frightfully, she managed to claw her way through particle board and fabric and wormy earth to break the surface, only to be smacked to death by an eighteen-wheeler as she trudged her way back home, unsteady and dehydrated, ankles twisting and spraining in the high heels she'd never worn in life but which had been slipped on her feet in death. He'd woken up, sweat-streaked and chest heaving many times in the days after her passing.

Their father, looking like he'd been pummeled with a bag of fruit, arrived at the table. His eyes were hollow, his skin the ashy color of an anemic pork chop. He rubbed at his face with the pads of his palms and yawned, shaking his head. Troy passed him a plate. He ate three bites of toast then tossed it back onto the plate, scattering crumbs across the porcelain before he stood and marched out of the house. Troy was the only one who followed.

The walk from the farmhouse to the golf course took five minutes; the morning was already sweating, dew clustered on the high grass, heat waving off the asphalt of the frontage road and the interstate beyond. The noise of cars zooming along the highway and the heavy breeze whistling through his ears gave Troy an excuse not to speak.

As usual, his father unlocked the concession stand and marched into the office, shutting the door behind him. Troy got to work wiping down the putters with sanitizing tissues, polishing their heads to glinting, placing the balls he'd left on the drying rack last night back into their slots in the metal dispenser so children could choose their favorite of six iridescent colors. He rummaged through the walk-in freezer for leftover ice cream, yanking the scoopers from the drying racks, restocking the waffle cones. They were on their last batch of churned ice cream, barely an inch left in the ten-gallon tub. Tim had no new milk to process and wheel over on the small ATV he used to haul gallons from the creamery over to the stand. There were no cows, no milk, hardly a shoppe.

Troy stood in the stand listening. The sound came up, as it had for several days straight now, in a sad, cresting wave: the blunted noise of his father's sobs, soft as the whoosh of the dishwasher at first, then rising as he lost control. Troy's stomach twisted. He closed his eyes and felt himself bobbing on his father's sorrow.

A school bus pulled into the lot minutes after Troy unhooked the chain draped over the entryway; he was hardly back in the stand before he heard the patter of dozens of kiddie footsteps.

His father leaned out of the office, groaning.

"Oh god," he said. "I forgot about the campers. Do we have anything in stock?"

Troy peered into the deep cooler where ice cream had once collected but was now empty aside from the coagulated condensation that had formed wavering ridges of porous ice. Troy nudged a finger at it and crumbles peeled off, scattering in the bottom. He looked back at his father and shook his head.

"Fuck. Okay." He disappeared back into the office, then emerged with a handful of bills. "Look, they paid a big group rate for twenty kids and five adults to do a round of eighteen each, followed by an ice cream party. I'm going to go buy some gallons from the Stop-n-Shop. I'll be back before they're done."

He watched his father dart past the first portion of the child horde. The kids ignored him, zooming and darting like field mice around the metal tables, some of them bouncing up and down, shouting with excitement toward the display of golf balls. Others shrieked about ice cream, banging their tiny splayed hands against the sneeze guard like it was a bass drum. They were dressed in identical yellow shirts with the name *Camp Oswego!* in bright blue Comic Sans; their counselors' shirts were the exact opposite, the neon yellow letters blurbing out from cotton stained the color of the Indian Ocean. One of them walked up to the window where Troy was slumped and staring at the kids.

It was Saul Fleishman. He was tan, his brown hair bleached to wheat by his days in the sun. The swirls of hair on his arms were golden flecks, and the t-shirt strained against his shoulders.

"Hey man."

"Hey," Troy said, standing up straight. "My dad explained."

"Golf and ice cream for the kids," Saul said.

"Well, they can each pick a club and a ball."

Saul let out a rip-roaring whistle that somehow had the power to stop all of the children at once, as if he'd cast a spell calcifying their joints into rock. He yelled some kind of camp chant and the kids fell into a pair of messy lines. Saul sauntered back to the window and, without a word, started pulling balls from the dispenser, a random arrangement, hauling a fistful of the small plastic kid-sized clubs.

Troy watched. Saul moved with a languid assurance, as if he was made of water that dripped and sloughed however it wanted. When he handed out the clubs and balls, two of the kids tried to swap, but Saul told them, voice stiff and hard as a two by four, to use the ones he'd given them. One of the children, a squeaky girl with wispy hair, said that her favorite color was pink, and that the boy she was trying to exchange with didn't want pink as much as he wanted her green.

Saul shook his head.

Troy's father squelched into the concession stand twenty minutes later while the first group of kids was rounding the sixth hole. He dragged two tubs of ice cream, one in each hand, and gestured for Troy to help him.

"Scoop it out into the tins."

"Why?"

"So it looks like ours."

"But it looks nothing like ours."

They stared at one another for a long moment, the only noise the raucous screaming of children as they thwacked at their golf balls.

"Let it melt a little," his father said, dropping the tubs with a snorty thump onto the concrete floor. He waved his hand and dashed into the office, slamming the door behind him. Troy looked out through the cashier window and watched the children laughing and stomping across the greens, dragging their plastic putters like rigid tails. The counselors kept score on printed grids the size of index cards, propping them on their thighs and scribbling with the stubby eraser-less pencils Troy kept stocked in a mesh cup next to the balls. Besides Saul, who was hawkishly barking for the kids in his group to maintain an orderly fashion, the counselors were letting the kids muck around however they liked, taking second and third whacks with their clubs before their balls had stopped rolling. One kid slid his along the ninth hole like a hockey puck, dribbling it all the way to the hole. Another he heard thump her ball so hard it flew into the murky pond tinged purplish green like an oil stain. Troy sighed and waited, holding out another ball before the counselor appeared, a sobbing seven-year-old following in her wake.

The first group of campers curled back around forty-five minutes later, bouncing with dizzy energy as they approached the eighteenth hole. Elodie stomped in then, stopping in the middle of the stand and planting her hands on her hips. She gestured toward the sweating tubs of ice cream.

"What are these?"

"A back-up plan," Troy said, gesturing toward the shuttered office.

Elodie sputtered her lips and charged over to the office door and banged on it. Troy trudged to the ice cream and hauled it onto the low counter behind the freezer. He pried open the vanilla, which had turned into a dense soup, loose enough that he could simply drive a spatula into one side and slide the entire mucky heap into one of the steel pans. Troy repeated the process with the chocolate while Elodie kept banging on the door, her right hand in a tight fist.

"Dad," she called out. "Open the door."

The kids at the eighteenth green shrieked and chirped. The hole was shaped like a long Skee-Ball chute, the upswerved area where the cup lay covered by a slanted metal grille. In order to win a free game, golfers had to shoot straight and true halfway up the incline; any shorter, higher, or off-center and the ball would get chunked into a low trough that fed into a box hidden beneath a trap door in the grass. A ball plunked into the hole would set off an electronic bell that would whir from the side of the concession stand and light up a police siren atop the hole's cage. One after another, the kids' balls zoomed up the ramp, clattering past the hole and banging around before settling into one of the chutes.

Elodie tapped Troy on the shoulder.

"He won't come out. He won't even say anything." Her eyes were wide, pupils dilated like she'd snorted cocaine. "Something's wrong."

Troy sighed. "I'm sure he's fine."

She stared. Troy huffed and marched to the office door, rapping with his knuckles. "Dad, come out. You're freaking out Elodie."

Troy heard nothing, no shuffling of papers, no squeak of the office chair. Usually their father played AM radio on a small hand-held he kept on a shelf, the talk show hosts' voices barely audible over the static that clogged the speakers, but even that was absent. Troy felt a little trampoline of nausea rise in his belly.

"He's probably sleeping," Troy said. "You know he doesn't at night, right?"

"Yeah, I hear the refrigerator door all the time."

"So he's napping."

"He snores. There's no snoring."

"I'm sure he's fine."

A cacophony of children's hands beating against the sneeze guard snapped Elodie and Troy to attention. Saul was standing behind the kids, arms folded over his bloat of a chest, saying nothing as the children screeched and moaned for their ice cream like a gang of rowdy football fans. Troy and Elodie began scooping, Troy managing the vanilla and Elodie the chocolate. The kids seemed to multiply like rabbits, clotting the space before the ice cream stand, many of them speeding through the final hole to take up their place in the queue.

When all the children were distracted by their ice cream cones, the counselors stepped up to the stand for their own. Saul was last, a bullish smirk on his face. He pulled off his reflective sunglasses and perched them on his head.

Standing in front of Elodie, he leaned over the guard and said, "I know that's store-bought. But don't worry. I won't say anything."

"Okay," she said.

"Sorry about the cows."

"How'd you know?" Troy said.

"Everybody knows."

"But how?"

"Just one of those things. It gets around." He took his cone and winked at Elodie. "Thanks." Some of the ice cream dribbled down his knuckles. Saul smeared it on the sneeze guard.

"Douchebag," Elodie murmured.

Troy watched Saul walk away, calves flexing like a beating heart.

As the bus pulled away, its air brakes farting noise into the air, Troy and Elodie turned back to their father's office. Troy, trying to forget Saul's leery gaze at Elodie, started pounding. She joined in, and they slammed at the door in tandem, non-stop, bashing their fists against the flimsy plywood until something, anything happened. They got into a steady, lengthy rhythm. Troy thought of Saul Fleishman. He thought of the cows. The dripping, grainy store-bought ice cream. The smell of cud. The wick-wack of golf clubs and balls.

Then, out of nowhere, the siren above the eighteenth hole went off, the bell letting out a whooping whine. They whirled around, the siren spinning and flaring its red glare into the spangle of the afternoon. At that same moment, the office door yawned open.

Frozen in his chair, Paul Buckingham's shoulders were stiff, as if caught on a hanger. He was staring toward the open doorway. Nothing was wrong with him, nothing noticeable aside from the utter stillness of his chest, the lifelessness of his eyes. Elodie shrieked, but all Troy could do was stare the cavernous shape of his father's mouth, rounded into an O as if trapped in the midst of letting out a low, vibrating moo.

Shark Boys

Unlike the rest of the athletes at Fairmont Country Day Academy, who wrapped themselves up in letterman jackets dotted with chevrons and medallions and obnoxious patches shaped like Missouri, the varsity swimmers donned sleek blue windbreakers with the words *Shark Boys* etched across the back in slanted black text, a vicious great white curled below, the team member's name riding in its hook-sharp teeth. There were no girls on the swim team, probably because the coach was a misogynist, but he never got called out because the team won the state championship year after year; kids moved from all over the country just to swim for Coach Baker.

The team was comprised of the school's twelve best swimmers, and they were treated like gods, the way most high schools idolize their football players. They were each broad-shouldered and muscular like models, tan and smooth-skinned and smelling like chlorine as if fresh from a surf at Big Sur. They shaved their underarms into cool, empty pits. Most of them were smart, in AP classes and presidents of one club or another. None of them worked after-school jobs; their parents were, one and all, rich. Each Shark Boy had his own BMW or Mercedes or Escalade, and they all parked in the same two rows right near the front entrance, every vehicle shiny with polish, capped with some kind of vanity license plate extolling a love of the back stroke or butterfly.

Their names were common knowledge, rolling off tongues with the ease of mnemonic devices. During Curtis Sutton's junior year, the squad included KJ Armour, Stewart Basso, Chris Dillard, Nick Hogan, Andrew Nixon, Michel Popudakis, Seth Tavers, Anthony Tillman, Derek Yanis, Ryan Zilke, and captain Phillip Mattox, who won three individual state medals in the breaststroke and freestyle as a sophomore the season prior. They were all nice, except for Andrew and Seth, who were Neanderthals with heads bigger than the doorways they walked through, boys who slapped cheerleaders on their asses, who shot spit wads across the room during lectures on the geography of Asia and pretended to fart during the frog dissection lab. The other Shark Boys were good and kind, especially Nick Hogan, who asked Becky Salavarti, who had Down syndrome, to go to Homecoming that year. But it was the team captain, Phillip, who Curtis couldn't stop staring at, unable to answer Ms. Partenheimer's questions about *Catcher in the Rye* or *The Collector* because he was busy gazing with untrammeled longing at the swimmer sitting studiously across the room, scribbling down in a notebook everything their teacher said, the gumdrop tip of his tongue protruding from his lips.

During meets, Curtis perched in the second row of the bleachers in the hothouse natatorium full of churning water and screeching teenagers. The cheerleaders led the crowd in a series of rah-rah, sis-boom-bah chants, though because of the slick tiled floor with its dangerous grout they skipped their usual dazzle of backflips and handsprings. Curtis sat next to his best friends, Brick Thomas and Danny Smithson, who spent the entirety of every meet lamenting the lack of female swimmers while ogling the cheerleaders in their tight knit uniforms, hair slick with humidity. Curtis, on the other hand, was always staring at the starting blocks, eyes glommed on the chiseled V shapes of the swimmers' lower torsos where lines of raised muscle disappeared into Spandex-tight swim trunks. Curtis ran cross country and had strong legs of his own, but he was in a war with his own upper body, his shoulders knobby and his chest flat no matter how much weight he pressed and pulled, heaved, and tossed; his hands were chapped and callused by dumbbells and battling ropes. He woke up sore all the time, muscles achy at the touch, tendons rippling with pain when he stretched or probed at his chest and back. But his body wouldn't grow. Unlike the Shark Boys, who had bodies like Hollywood actors who pretended to be teenagers, Curtis actually looked like a teenager.

His favorite event was the fifty-meter freestyle, when the bulky swimmers thrashed through the water with all their might, churning the aquamarine surface into a frothy, bubbling mess of white. Arms and legs flashed and flailed, waves cresting in such sprightly plumes that sometimes fans in the first row caught sprinkles, like they were sitting in the splash zone at Sea World. He watched, silently willing Phillip Mattox to success, and every time he won Curtis gave a quiet *whoop* along with the rest of the Fairmont fans, spending too much of the cheering time stealing quick glimpses at Phillip's body as he pulled himself from the pool, hamstrings glistening with sluicing water that caught in the divots of his knees.

In late October, Fairmont hosted the last dual meet of the regular season, against their rival Mary Institute. The stands were packed, kids in Fairmont purples and greens, the small cadre from the visiting team huddled in a corner near the starting blocks. Curtis and Brick and Danny had been given miniature pom-poms to chuff and swirl in the air. Brick brought a foam finger that he slid onto his left hand and kept poking at Curtis. Fairmont won the two relays that started the meet, but Mary Institute capitalized in the backstroke, Fairmont's weakest event. Other than that, the day went to the home team, which racked up enough points that the fifty free was meaningless.

Except nothing was meaningless to the Shark Boys.

The eight swimmers shot off the blocks in a surge at the bleep of the electronic bell. Curtis lost track of Phillip's body in the center lane; his angle of vision was sharp at the far end of the bleachers, and the plumes of water splashing up made a curtain that blocked his view of the stretching arms, the pulsing lats, the fluttering calves. When they made their single turn at the end of the twenty-five meter pool, he couldn't tell who was in the lead.

The crowd's screeching increased in pitch in the final ten meters, a single clump of indistinct noise. Curtis wondered if the swimmers could hear it through the pumping of their hearts, their ragged breaths, the swish and swash of the water. Was it like a thumping bass, maybe, or the dizzy blur of cicadas chirping in the summer?

The best freestylers, in the center, were all bunched, bodies stretched to hit the pool's edge. Four of them bobbed up in near-tandem, ripping off their occluded goggles and suctioned-on swim caps, twisting around to look up at the scoreboard while they treaded water. The audience stared, too, with bated breath.

Everyone except Curtis, who was looking at Phillip, and thus looking at the water, and was the only one who noticed that the surface was still bubbling and churning even though the swimmers had stopped moving. The official results came up—Phillip Mattox winning the race by two tenths of a second—and the crowd cheered. At the same time, Michel Popudakis, bobbing in lane eight, let out a shriek and scrambled from the water.

He was followed quickly by the others, Nick Hogan, Ryan Zilke, and finally Phillip, along with the four swimmers from Mary Institute. The Shark Boys' cheers died on their lips, and the crowd, which had been clapping and pumping fists—Brick's foam finger waggling like a buzzy antenna—froze as the swimmers evacuated the churning, bubbling, *boiling* water, slapping at their wet limbs.

Their bodies were blistered and scalded. Coach Baker barked orders. An assistant coach slipped and skidded across the slick floor toward a first aid kit mounted against the wall, flinging it open and staring at the contents before grabbing up every tube of ointment, box of gauze, and packet of tablets he could carry in his basketed arms. Another darted toward a stack of folded towels, flinging them toward the boys whose skin was flaring with heat, the water coursing off them so hot it steamed against their peeling flesh. The athletic trainers for each team grabbed at the burned swimmers, trying to pull them toward the locker room. Parents stumbled down the bleachers, demanding access to their sons. Girlfriends shrieked. The cheerleaders covered their mouths, some of them bawling at the sight of so much gorgeous, injured skin.

Both teams and their staffs disappeared into the tunnel leading to the locker room. The crowd murmured confusion, disbelief. The water had settled to a steady simmer, bubbles popping and steam rising from the surface as if it was a huge pot of aqua soup. A few intrepid fans tip-toed to the edge of the pool and lowered hands and feet toward the hot surface, then shied away. One soccer player feigned shoving another in, the victim twisting around and punching his assaulter's shoulder. Parents pulled small children to their sides as they vacated the bleachers, taking sharp, unsure glances toward the water.

Curtis, Brick, and Danny trundled away from the pool in silence, dumping their pom-poms in a trash can next to the concession stand, where three kids in identical t-shirts advertising the athletic boosters club watched the crowd disperse. That night, Curtis barely touched his dinner, ignoring his parents' exhortations for him to eat the pasta primavera that his mother made because she knew he loved it. He was trapped in a looping tape of the pool bubbling up into a scorching frenzy, his brain zooming in on the blistered, popping backs of the Shark Boys like they were pigs being seared on spits. Phillip Mattox's tan skin had peeled away in horrible pink strips, his legs throbbing with agony as he stumbled toward the locker room. Curtis trembled when he went to bed that night, haunted by the nightmarish pustules had seen rising on the backs of Phillip's legs.

Curtis slipped into the hospital burn unit at the tail end of visiting hours on a blustery, chilled Sunday, the leaves on the maples dazzling the grass with reds and ambers in heavy heaps. He skittered past reception after meekly asking which room housed Phillip Mattox, the nurse on duty blinking up at him and offering him a wan smile when she saw the nervous jitter of his left leg. She pointed down the hall but said Phillip might be sleeping. All of the injured swimmers had been drowsy, bodies gunky with morphine and skin plastered with Plexaderm, IVs pumping them full of antibiotics.

"He may not really know you're here."

"Will he be okay?"

A new, sorrowful smile blossomed on her face. "I can't really say."

The hallway was brightened by harsh fluorescents that buzzed like a hive. An abandoned wheelchair was shoved against a propped-open door. Curtis passed the rooms where Michel and Ryan and Nick were holed up, uneaten trays of hospital jello curled away from their beds. Phillip's room was the last one in the ward, stationed next to a supply closet and second nurse's station where a plump woman in fuschia scrubs was humming and rummaging around a cluttered desk. As Curtis slipped into Phillip's room, her phone rang.

He was asleep, a monitor blipping out the steady rhythm of his heart. Even in repose, swaddled in a confetti-colored hospital gown, Phillip Mattox was a statuesque god, the swimmer's build shining through the forest of machines and tubes surrounding him like a plastic throne. Curtis walked to the side of the bed. Phillip looked like he was laid in state, flat on his back, arms down by his sides. If it weren't for the up and down heave of his wide chest and the slight flutter of his lips as he breathed, Curtis would have thought him dead.

He didn't touch Phillip, though he felt the desperate tugging desire to press his fingers to his splayed hand where an IV needle emerged along the back, trailing up his wrist and forearm. To feel that smooth flesh, the wrinkly knuckles, the ligaments laced with the hinted blue worms of veins. They weren't friends, exactly; every year, the varsity teams got together for an end-of-term dinner where letters and polished trophies were handed out. Teams were encouraged to split up, and none led the way quite like the Shark Boys. Last year, Curtis and his parents had sat with Phillip and his sister and mother, the boys next to each other, making light references to their shared biology class and how ridiculously easy the final exam had been for both of them despite Mrs. Stegner's insane multiple choice questions that might have more than one correct answer and you were expected to find all of them. They'd laughed and smiled at one another and Phillip had offered up hearty applause when Curtis was called up to receive a medal for his third place finish at the state cross country championships; Phillip had even clapped Curtis on the back when he sat back down. Phillip leaned in and looked at the medal, his beachy smell filling Curtis's nostrils.

Curtis had gone home that night with a tireless aching warmth in his joints. He'd thought, *Maybe.* Just maybe there'd be more. That the glint he'd seen in Phillip Mattox wasn't just kindness but want, the same unfulfilled desire Curtis felt whenever he looked at the new leader of the Shark Boys. But during the last days of the year, Phillip acted as if the dinner had never happened. The shimmering smile was dulled back to normal, and although Curtis received hellos and head nods, friendly greetings when they worked together in small group discussions in English class, nothing compared to the dinner.

Curtis backed out of the hospital room, keeping his eyes on Phillip's resting body. He was not sure why he came, what he planned to do. He paused at the doorway, curling his fingers around the frame, dipping backward and forward, then finally retreated into the hospital.

The wheelchair was gone.

Practice was canceled. Test after test was run on the pool's water, its filtration system, the boilers, even the heating and cooling elements in the air conditioning units. No one could find anything wrong.

Coach Baker updated the school's website about the injured swimmers' healing process. The boys weren't getting worse, but they weren't getting better. Their bodies were covered in boils, as if they'd been hit by infectious disease rather than burned. To stay in shape for districts, the unharmed Shark Boys went to the local recreation center, passes purchased by the school.

And then it happened again: the unharmed Shark Boys were tooling around in the lap pool with its dippy plastic lane markers and bored lifeguards sitting in lighthouse-shaped lookout chairs, blitzing their whistles at kids in water wings to slow down. They were practicing their form, lazing through sets under the disinterested eye of one of the team managers, a chubby wannabe swimmer who followed Coach Baker around with a clipboard noting times and PRs. No one noticed when bubbles began popping on the water's edge, homing toward the center.

Andrew and Seth were blessed by fortune again, each taking a breather when the water started to warm, arms draped over the rings of the lane dividers. They clambered out quick as silverfish, dashing the balls of their feet against the slippery, splashed cement border. Rather than yelling for the others to escape the heat they slapped at their skin where they had been barely burnt. Anthony Tillman was hit the worst, scalded across his back and sides as he pinwheeled his arms around doing the backstroke. He was trapped in the pool's dead center when the bubbling grew to its greatest intensity and by the time he had dragged himself to the edge he was in such pain he had to be hoisted out by Derek and Chris, who were themselves hobbled by the blisters already forming over their shoulder blades. Stew Basso had been in the bathroom and became the last untouched Shark Boy.

The day after KJ, Chris, Derek, and Anthony were admitted to the burn unit, Nick, Michel, Ryan, and Phillip were moved to intensive care, their bodies saved from infection but still coursing with blisters along the epidermis. Nurses applied salving creams three times a day, and their morphine doses were reduced so they were conscious. Curtis skipped his last-period study hall on a Tuesday afternoon, where a bored math teacher never took attendance, to visit Phillip.

In a different hall in a different end of the building, the intensive care unit was a somber yet noisy place. Machines of all sorts blipped in muffled tones through closed doors. Doctors fluttered, loafers clopping on the linoleum like horse hooves. Nurses unfurled stethoscopes and pushed crash carts when patients dipped and dived toward death. Curtis stood at the reception desk, watching the buzz and chatter. Finally a nurse noticed him, the mint green of her scrubs matching her eye shadow. She smiled and asked how she could help him, the mania suddenly gone from her face, the frown that had been etched across her forehead as she reviewed case information erased like so much movable sand.

He told her, and she pointed the way.

"He's awake, I think," she said. "You kids have been keeping them company nicely."

Curtis felt a curling stab in his stomach as he walked toward Phillip's room, like he hadn't eaten all day. His gut moaned.

He thought about skipping out. Dashing back down the hallway with its cream walls and charts hanging in opaque file holders. Past the nurses, to the elevator bay, down to his car and home. But he took a deep breath, unhitched his uniform tie and untucked his shirt. When he reached Phillip's room, he knocked on the cracked door and stuck his head in.

Phillip was reading *Crime and Punishment*, their newest assignment in Ms. Partenheimer's class. Studious as always. He tented the book on his stomach and looked at Curtis.

"Hey."

"Hi," Curtis said. "Umm."

"Next in line, huh?"

"You know about that?"

"Christy Yamato is a nice girl but she's not so sensitive about sharing her motives. You have a late study hall?"

"This seemed better than sitting under the eye of Mr. Blanco."

"He does usually smell like processed cheese late in the afternoon. It's worse in the hot months, though."

Curtis chuckled. He shoved his hands in his pockets.

"You gonna come in or what?"

"You look a lot better."

Phillip shrugged, his hospital gown catching on the scratchy pillow. "I feel okay, but the doctors can't explain why the burns aren't healing." He tugged at his sleeve, pulling it up along his shoulder. The skin was mottled with pustules.

Curtis stepped closer. "Do they hurt?"

"Only if someone touches them."

"I won't."

But he wanted to. Phillip let the sleeve fall back in place. Curtis missed that curved, punchy shoulder already. He had dreamed of the swimmer's skin many times, the flesh chilled and tight from the chlorine and salt that seeped across it when he arced through his laps.

Curtis settled for laying his hand on the rail of Phillip's bed that caged him like a sedated animal.

"So," Phillip said.

"So." Curtis glanced at the clock. He'd signed up for a thirty-minute block, though he didn't think anyone would know if he left early, slinking back through the hallways with their smells of antiseptic spray and bodily fluid.

"Have you started yet?" Phillip said, flicking a finger at *Crime and Punishment.*

Curtis shook his head.

"The names are long. A bit confusing at times. Russians, I guess."

"Yeah."

"You don't have to stay, you know," Phillip said.

"It's okay."

"Most people haven't stayed. I think we freak them out."

"You don't freak me out."

And then that smile, the gregarious, burning grin that he'd seen at the awards dinner, was back, finally, six months later. It was purled with a calm, thoughtful happiness like Phillip was remembering a dream of flight. He closed and then opened his eyes and reached a hand up to the center of his hospital gown, tugging down the collar to reveal his blistered chest.

"These don't hurt as much," he said, tapping at a pale strip. "Do you want to feel?"

Curtis felt his mouth fill with gum, a chewy resistance to speech. Phillip stared up at him, eyes owlish, yanking harder at the flimsy material. Curtis peeled his hand from the metal of the bedrail and let it drift upward, fingers scanning past Phillip's hip and forearm and finally stopping at his sternum. Curtis lowered it slowly, like a feather drifting downward, and then connected with Phillip's flesh.

He'd expected pliancy and heat but was instead greeted by a cool stiff resistance where the scar tissue had formed over the burn. He tickled his fingers along the strip of flesh and Phillip let out a small squeak of noise. Curtis blanched, trying to tuck away the shiver pushing against him from the inside.

Phillip laid his hand atop Curtis's, heavy like it had hardened into steel.

"Your hand feels nice there. When the doctors and nurses touch me, it isn't nice. But this is." He shut his eyes and let out a long sigh. Curtis felt a throb go up and down his arm. It trailed into his shoulder, along his clavicle and sternum, down into his gut. Phillip did not move, but Curtis could feel the just-so lift of his body as he breathed, steady and slow. He stood there a long time, the tick and whirl of the machinery surrounding them the only noise. Curtis made no move to leave. He was willing to stand there for the rest of his life.

The boils brought the end of the Shark Boys. No other swimmers at Fairmont were willing to get in the pool or don the blue windbreakers, worried they were of curses and ghouls and scalding water. Stewart Basso quit the team and was even afraid of showers. Although they'd barely been burned, Andrew and Seth flaunted the wispish scars on their calves and arms. Because no one would swim in regional competition, Coach Baker wrote to the MSHSAA and announced Fairmont's forfeiture.

The boys who had been scalded felt fine, eventually, even though the boils remained along their backs and stomachs and thighs. They were discharged, all eight, once their bodies were stable internally, armed with prescription-strength creams and pills that they hauled into their crusty bathrooms and stored under the sink. The looks they received were piteous, empathetic instead of awed. Girls tried to touch their mottled flesh but shirked away at the last second.

Curtis and Phillip started slipping into the boys' bathroom near the natatorium, abandoned by everyone except the janitorial staff after a rumor swirled that it was cursed; kids were sure the sinks carried the same boiling water that had the Shark Boys. They entered in silence, slipping through the door with a careful quiet. Phillip would uncoil his tie and pull off his shirt and Curtis would wander around him, pressing his hands to the scars, the flesh churned like macerated fruit. Then came down Phillip's jeans, and Curtis swept his cooling fingers along Phillip's warm thighs, tight calves, the rocky tops of his feet. After, Phillip dressed without a word. Curtis waited, following him out minutes later, turning left while Phillip went right, Curtis headed to world history while Phillip slipped into chemistry. Phillip never looked back, never gave himself away, but from time to time Curtis turned just enough to catch the fluttered back of Phillip's head, the tight hairline high on his neck, the tweetering bit of muscle stretching on his throat and upper back. Curtis watched him greet his friends, no one else in the world aware of the feel of his pebbled skin, the chilly hardness on his scars and splotches. He would wait until Phillip turned a far corner and disappeared, then walk on, his hands throbbing with want and knowledge. Curtis wanted more than anything to be burnt up, crisped into hardly anything so he could be molded and touched too.

Glass Children

The Schaumbergs were the local athletic stars. Ben played football and baseball; his younger sister, Katy, my age, excelled at field hockey and soccer. He had idol-gold skin and sprinted through his backyard shirtless, shoving the weight sled his father bought for him for Christmas one year. I watched him from my bedroom window, high on the second story of our house. As he ran, the muscles in his lower back straining, his shoulder blades popped with more lines than a map. Katy was pale, dots of freckles spattered all along her warm thighs and porcelain face. She would stand on their back deck in cross trainers, jumping rope before dribbling a soccer ball, slapping it against the back of their garage. The Schaumbergs were Sicilian or Egyptian or something, eyelashes thick like they plastered them with mascara, chins cleft. He buzzed his black hair; hers fell to her shoulders, usually held up in a ponytail. Ben looked just like his father, Katy her mother.

Until the day the hail started, neither seemed to know I existed.

In July, Missouri air was hot, but the night of the hail a freak cold front barged in, dropping the temperature as well as a thunderous clatter that woke me at three in the morning. I looked out my bedroom window, where the quarter-sized globs of hail gathered on the ground. The glass was cool to the touch, and I checked it for little spiderweb cracks, but it was smooth as ever.

Most Saturdays, Ben went to summer football practice no later than seven in the morning, so Katy had the backyard to herself, where she practiced her traps, switching from her soccer ball to her field hockey stick and back. But that morning, neither of the Schaumbergs was outside; I was usually woken by the roar of the clunky pickup truck Ben had been given for his seventeenth birthday in February, but this morning I was roused by a strange blue haze streaming through my window.

I looked out and dragged a breath. Everything was covered in a sheet of transparent ice: the cherries on the tree in the backyard were wrapped in such a thick coat that they hung like Christmas ornaments; the sharp edges of Ben's weight sled were rounded like a couch. I dashed downstairs and peered through the living room bay window: a tipped-over tricycle in the yard across the street was an uneven, mutant igloo. Mr. Donaldson, who lived catty-corner to us, kept his dog Percival's wooden doghouse in his side yard, and the doorway was blocked by a thick slab. A trio of songbirds that must have been caught out in the storm were frozen solid on the thickest branch of the crab apple tree in our front yard, one of them wings aflutter, the first failed beatings of flight.

My parents came to stand behind me. Dad was in boxer shorts and a t-shirt, Mom in a velveteen robe that showed off her honey skin. They each pressed a hand to one of my shoulders, Dad squeezing my limp muscles too hard. The sun was shining and the glass in the window was warm; the trees were still green and lush. I was about to open the front door, but my mom protested, insisting we check the news first, but the television didn't work. The phone lines, my father discovered when he picked up our cordless, were dead. I wasn't surprised; the cables running between the poles were chained in the ice, drooping in waxy, stretchy smiles.

But the doorbell worked, and so did the toaster. My mother discovered the former when she wanted to crisp up some rye; the latter we learned when it ding-donged while we ate.

My parents sipped coffee. "Praise the lord!" my father said when the Keurig worked,

I answered the door. It took a while, but I managed to yank it open. A sheet of ice, blue and surreal, stood between me and them, but I knew exactly who was on the blurred other side: the Schaumbergs.

Ben, standing in front, tried to say something, but his voice was muddled like he was under water. I held up a hand, one finger extended, hoping it didn't look like I was flipping him off. I yelled for them to hang on, then rushed into the garage, my parents watching me dart through the kitchen. I found a tiny sledgehammer and ran back inside. My parents were still frozen, blinking at me with bemused smiles on their faces.

I told them who was at the door as I passed, as if this would explain why I was behaving like a Tasmanian devil.

"Stand back!"

The vague blobs of the Schaumbergs shuffled and distorted behind the ice, shrinking just so.

I took a swing. A small chip of ice clinked off, melting into invisible condensation on the hardwood floor. Tiny etches of white extended from the blow's center.

"This might take a second," I said, thankful they couldn't see the blush in my cheeks.

I was sweating by the time I managed to punch through. Ben and Katy stepped back to let the ice hit the front porch, which was also covered in a sleek layer of blue, as if someone had vacuum-sealed it in tinted Saran wrap. The Schaumbergs stared at me.

"Hi," I said, the hammer dangling in my right hand.

"I just shouldered my way out our front door," Ben said. He was wearing a tank top, and his left arm was bruised. He rubbed at it. "Maybe was a bad idea."

"What's happening?" Katy asked. She was usually stoic and strong. When she did speak, she echoed confidence. She was really good at math, had taken pre-calculus as a sophomore last year and had already taken the AP American History test, scoring a five. I'm pretty sure underclassmen weren't supposed to be allowed to take the test, but her dad had made a big donation to the Athletic Boosters, so the Schaumbergs could do just about whatever they wanted.

But now Katy looked pinched, punched inward.

"Our parents are out of town," Ben said. He explained that they were at their house at the Lake of the Ozarks; Ben couldn't go because of two-a-days, and Katy had planned to go to a big party tonight, one that, of course, I had heard nothing about.

"Can we come in?" Katy said.

"Yeah," I said, sweeping the front door open to its full length. "Please."

The Schaumbergs picked their way across the front porch in dainty, careful steps.

"I ate ass two feet out our door," Ben said. His yellow tank top made his gold skin look even darker. I could see the blurry smudge of his underarm hair at the juncture of muscle beneath his armpit.

They sat in the living room, where I explained the television wasn't working.

"Ours either," Katy said. "Couldn't put on CNN."

We sat in silence, the Schaumbergs squashed together on the love seat like an awkward couple, me drowning in the matching recliner, unsure of what to say. I tossed out some inane comment about the weather, which miraculously got Ben going.

"I don't get it," he said. "It's like, balls hot outside, and yet there's ice everywhere. Explain that. Someone." He looked from Katy to me and back, an incredulous, eggy look on his face like we were master meteorologists who refused to share information that was obvious to the two of us. "Ice, like, melts in warm weather, but that shit ain't doing anything."

I was saved by my mother, who whisked into the room and said hello to the Schaumbergs with an affable kindness, immediately snapping into helpful, worried adult mode. She asked about their parents, then inquired as to whether they were hungry (they were not) or thirsty (Ben accepted the offer of a glass of milk, Katy some water). When she brought the drinks she started on a lengthy communique, catching up on how they were spending their summer, doing everything she could to avoid talking about the wonky weather. She slipped in an invitation for them to stick around as long as they wanted, for lunch and dinner even, if they'd like that. Both Schaumbergs nodded. They weren't going anywhere.

Ben and Katy followed me into the back yard after we bashed out the sheen of ice blocking the sliding door. The sun was shining, hot and round as ever, the air tumid as if spewed out of a pre-heated oven. But the cherry trees were inflexible, the back deck as slick as a skating rink.

"Weird," I said.

Katy marched into the yard, taking care on the composite decking. She squelched her toes against the spikes of grass with a careful uncertainty, as if worried she might puncture the ball of her foot. But once she'd placed one foot down with ginger slowness, she turned back to me and Ben.

"It kind of tickles," she said.

Ben followed her, and I watched the Schaumberg siblings melt into childhood, prickling their feet against the icy grass and laughing with one another, their cheeks rounding with dimples. I kept looking from the one to the other: at Ben's powered, hulking arms that reached up to pinch at a thin, frozen bough from the tree, then Katy's graceful, lithe legs, the modest but still present curve of her chest. Both of them were like magnets, pulling my eyeballs toward their strong, well-manicured skin. I felt like I would short-circuit.

Katy waved for me to follow them into the yard. She bent down and picked up a fallen leaf ensconced in ice. When I joined them in the yard, she held it out to me. It was light, as if the ice was an illusion, a weightless dressing. I took it in my hand; the ice didn't melt. Katy picked up another leaf and crushed it between her fingers. I did the same. We let the shards dribble through our hands like sand.

Cell service was down, as was the internet. That afternoon, Ben mentioned wanting to work out, and my father told him about an old bench and some dusty weights he kept in our basement, so the Schaumberg kids tutted down the creaky steps into the musty room. I followed them, shushing my father before he could say a word about not remembering having ever seen me do a pushup in his life.

Our basement was filled with crumbling boxes stuffed with Christmas ornaments, old bedding, electronic equipment my dad inherited from his father that he couldn't bring himself to get rid of. The space was a big square, unfinished, with the water heater and furnace in the dead center. My mother had set down a few throw rugs in one corner, along with an old tube-back tv and a lumpy brocade-covered couch, thinking that I would use it to entertain my friends. That plan, however, was shot by the moldy smell of the basement and the fact that I didn't have enough friends.

I rooted through a bin filled with old tennis racquets, basketballs, and a Bocce set, and produced a half-deflated soccer ball for Katy. She blinked at it and offered some thanks before dribbling it to an empty corner and gently sweeping it toward the wall; it made a sad ricochet and slumped back toward her. I called up the stairs for my father to look in the garage for the air pump for his bicycle.

"You work out?" Ben asked me as he settled himself on the bench. It creaked under his weight.

"Sometimes."

"How much you press?" He gestured toward the stack of thick weight plates. They were plastic, filled with sand, bulbous and bloated.

"Well, uh, it's been a while. I'm not sure."

He raised an eyebrow.

The Schaumbergs built up a haze of sweat for an hour. Katy, after my father came downstairs holding aloft the bicycle bump in triumph, dribbled in place and did toe taps, her feet scruffing the top of the soccer ball as she bounced from one leg to the other. Ben loaded up the iron bar and blasted out bench presses and bicep curls. He held one of the heavy discs to his chest and extended his arms in and out. I struggled through some pushups. He showed me how to do front raises. Katy asked me to help her practice her footwork against an opponent.

"Just try to take the ball from me," she said.

"Okay."

My mother snuck some bottled water down to us, leaving it on the bottom step like a peace offering. We glugged the liquid down. Ben's chest heaved, his clavicle dense with sweat. Katy's hair was plastered to her forehead. They both glowed. I drooped. While the Schaumbergs were still going strong, looking like models in the background of a fitness video, I was hacking up my left lung, a deep cramp punching at my right side. I sprawled myself on the couch and stared at the cement wall, webbed with tiny cracks, listening while Katy chuffed and chunk-chunked the ball against the wall. Ben clanged the weights up and down.

They tromped across the yard to take showers before dinner. We ate in a stoic, awkward silence, the five of us crammed at our small kitchen table because my father had let junk mail and notes for his fantasy baseball league overrun the dining room table. I sat squished at one of the corners, Katy on my left and Ben on my right. They hunched over their food, Ben inhaling gargantuan bites of his soft shell tacos, his jaw seeming to unhinge like a python's. When he chewed, I could see the flex of the sharp, strong bones in his face. Katy thanked our parents for the food and for letting them use our basement, Ben nodding and grunting in agreement. My mom and dad smiled, glanced at me, then kept eating, shoveling pico and black beans into their mouths. I spread my own food around in a gluey mess.

My mom insisted that they stay the night. She booted me from my bed so Ben could sleep there while Katy took the guest room. I would camp out on the living room sofa, using extra blankets from the linen closet. I was wrestling around, trying to clunk my body into a comfortable position when I heard a plastering thwack on the bay window.

The hail was back.

I was sitting in the bay window, staring out at the darkness, hail clattering against the glass with such vehement plonking I was sure the window would shatter, when I heard the whine of the stairs

I turned. Katy was at the bottom, Ben halfway up. They both looked stricken, as though my mother's pulled chicken had poisoned them.

"Can't sleep?" I said.

"It sounds like someone's playing the bongo drums next to my head," Ben said.

"Yeah, the insulation isn't great in my room."

They padded down. Katy tucked herself up into the bay window opposite me, smelling like lilacs. Ben was shirtless, his muscles glimmering silver in the ambient light from a streetlamp that had survived the ice, power still coursing through its wires. It felt like a tiny, torchlit miracle.

I tried not to stare at either of them, the boggling delicacy of Katy's hard, strong ankles, the clean arch of her foot, the strip of taut skin visible where her tank top didn't reach the crinkled band of her shorts. Ben's accordion of ab muscles, the curled trail of black hair dribbling from his belly button—a hard outie, like a fleshy bottlecap—down into his boxer shorts, the hard lines of his quads. They each radiated a suave strength, something easy and inborne. My muscles ached from the hard yards in the basement.

Absently, I reached a hand up to my chest, massaging my left pec. Sour pain lit up all the way to my underarm.

We watched the hail in silence. In the shadowy darkness the powdery balls clogged the yard, building up and up in a steady sea that would blanket everything come morning. The only noise was the pounding of the hail on every surface of the house, the street, the calluna bushes. It outstripped everything, the sound of our breaths, the *schiff* of skin against the carpet, the antsy thrum of my bewildered heart.

Night daggered its way into my chest like an eel. I woke up needing to pee, but I shoved the tingly, biting feel in my bladder aside. The hail was thundering against the walls of the house like drumbeats.

I slithered upstairs.

Katy had shut the guest room door, but Ben had left mine open, a sardine can twirl of moonlight slipping out through the jamb. I padded down to the room with a careful, ninja drawl. The beat of the hail was thick, but when I got close I could still hear: Ben Schaumberg was sobbing.

In a movie, I'd have gone to him, thrown myself on his half-naked body and planted my lips on his, drawing his sorrow out like a weaver's mistake. Instead, I stood there, my feet going to ice, my chest impaling itself on its own breath, listening as Ben Schaumberg raveled and spasmed in sorrow. I felt something cut into my side like a slicing knife. I looked up, and there was Katy, a hand on my hip. She pressed the other, pointer finger up, to her lip. We backed away.

"He's sensitive," Katy said. "Smart, but no one wants him to be."

She stared at me.

"Don't tell anyone."

The Schaumberg parents didn't come home Sunday. Phones still weren't working and the collective wisdom was that the roads were too wick-slick for any sane driver to attempt travel, especially someone zigzagging up the windy curls and hairpin turns of state highways MM, TT, and 54 from Tan-Tar-A. Ben said his father would never attempt such a drive facing even the most minor weather obstacle.

"One time," Ben said, "we stayed down there an entire extra day because it was drizzling. Dad said light rain pulls up the oils embedded in asphalt and makes the road deceptively slick." He rolled his eyes. I looked for the glassy reflection of the previous night but saw nothing.

We were munching on granola bars because the electricity had finally crapped out sometime in the night. Everything in my body hurt, and I was in desperate want of a soda, a glass of milk, anything but the lukewarm tap water my mother set out, but she was insistent that the refrigerator remain shut up like a bank vault to keep the lunchmeats and leftovers from spoiling.

The day lazed by. When the Schaumbergs asked, again, to use the basement to work out, I begged off, finding it hard to imagine how I could possibly hoist up even the five-pound weights from the floor. Katy insisted, tugging on my arm while I languished on the couch.

"But we'd have to take cold showers afterward," I moaned.

"A light lift is good for sore muscles," Ben said. "Come on." He went so far as to cuff a hand around my arm, massaging his fingers into my noodly muscle. I bit my tongue.

I let Ben drag me through a series of curls and body weight squats and overhead presses, my lactic-laden muscles shrieking. Katy did jumping jacks and football runs, more toe touches on the soccer ball. Ben put me through bench step-ups and triceps dips that made my arms wobble. We stood facing one another for skater jumps and then borrowed the soccer ball, tossing it to one another and squatting down in tandem. He had to shove me up the stairs when we were finished.

My father tramped onto the back deck and started up the charcoal grill after knocking its lid loose from its blue case of ice. He convinced my mom to let him open the deep freezer in the garage, assuring her that he'd only let out the smallest blip of cold air. She acquiesced when he pointed out that it was either open up something or begin the slow grinding process of starvation. I didn't mention that the pantry was stocked with plenty of dry cereal and peanut butter and bread.

While my father warmed up the grill, I laid down on the deck still slick with ice.

"What are you doing?" he asked.

"Cooling off."

"Quite the workouts they've been putting you through."

"I'm dying."

"It's good for you."

"How is death good for me?"

"Don't be so dramatic."

I swished my arms and legs like I was making a snow angel, but when I stood—nearly slipping and crashing more than once—it was as if I hadn't laid there at all, the ice uniform and unblemished. I felt like a ghost.

Phone service came back that night, signaled by both of the Schaumbergs' iPhones blasting out a smattering of notifications: missed calls, texts, Instagram comments, Snapchats. I watched their fingers scramble along the screens. Ben listened to his voicemail. Something flickered in his eyes. I glanced his way, wondering what would reflect back, but he didn't say anything.

Mom fidgeted through one of the drawers in the kitchen, saying she was pretty sure the Schaumbergs had given her the number for their lake house once. She eventually produced an old Post-It note, the sticky end clumped with dust and stray hairs, crinkled from its time smothered by scissors and a Swingline stapler and a pair of wooden rulers.

"Aha!" she declared, holding the paper up like a winning lottery ticket.

No one answered when she dialed.

"But at least the line works now," she said.

"Their voicemail," Ben finally admitted, "said they were going to try to come back tonight. Now I can't get either of them to answer."

"Oh, sweetie." My mom pressed a hand to his shoulder.

The Schaumbergs took up residence in the bay window that night, ignoring my parents' exhortations that they should get some sleep. Ben sat where I'd been. I studied his face: translucent and unmoving and filled with secrets. I stared out the window with them. We said nothing as we watched the hail come down again, blasting against the already-thick curtain of ice that had curved over the window. They were waiting, hoping, for the headlights of their parents' car to come churning through the night, but I think even they knew they were waiting for nothing.

Katy started crying, a silent diphthong of noise that burped up when her chest caught. Ben snaked his hand out and cupped it over her ankle. I watched the rise and fall of his ribs.

They sat for hours, carved into the window like statues. When the moon shoved through, their skin was tinted blue. I knew I should either go to bed or go to them. But what to say? What to do? Lay a hand on each of the Schaumbergs, pierce the shells forming around them with my warmth, my welcoming? What hope did I have of moving them?

My breathing went shallow and sharp; the muscles around my ribs were sore, shooting me with a hot tingle at every inhale. The hail kept falling, the Schaumbergs kept staring. The air was solid. In a flash, it came to me: they would leave in the morning, stake out to find their parents even if it meant their own ends. Unless I did something now, here, to keep them with me.

My head swam. The Schaumbergs stared out, frozen.

Everything was icy and uncertain.

Terrarium

The bugs came during Nyle's third week at Hottie House. He was in the Jacuzzi, body pressed to the faux-marble liner while Bailey kissed his neck, the football player's hands dancing along Nyle's lats and hips with a slow, careful ease. They had the same body type even though Nyle had never run a cross route or scored a touchdown in his life, building his lean mass through hard hours in the gym, clobbering his body with Romanian deadlifts, Zottman curls, and front squats. Bailey was bigger. A trail of hair drizzled down from his belly button and a blond thatch sprouted between his pecs where Nyle's torso was shaved clean. Bailey never seemed nervous or apprehensive like Steve and Dom and Adam were when they did duo shows. He never laughed nervously or made jokes about touching another guy's dick for money. His voice was sweet and deep and full of seductive ichor, and sometimes, like in the moment before the bugs descended, Nyle wondered if Bailey, too, had lied on his application, claiming that he was totally, absolutely, one hundred percent straight.

Because that was the whole premise of Hottie House. Five dudes, straight hetero athletes with bomb-ass bodies, were willing to be filmed naked, jerkin' the gherkin at all hours of the day in all sorts of wacky ways, interacting with fans in live chats, filming close-ups with handhelds, taking directions from the overly enthused producer who filmed on a Canon FX 300. Their straightness was key, the Hottie House empire built on the premise that these college guys who loved to pound pussy were swinging wildly out of their comfort zone for the pleasure of their hopelessly horny gay onlookers who wanted to see buff dudes with sculpted pecs and shoulders like grenades kiss and lick and tug at one another. They lived together in an LA bungalow way nicer than anything twenty-one-year-olds from places like Duluth, Paducah, and Lynchburg would ever be able to afford on their own. Real granite countertops, brass and gold sink fixtures, chandeliers, a carriage house and in-ground pool, every mattress nestled in a sleigh bed frame and decked out with Dreamsacks silk sheets and plump pillows. The couches were patent leather, the televisions high-def.

Bailey saw the bugs first. He was nibbling at Nyle's earlobe when he pulled away.

"Dude." Bailey lifted a hand from Nyle's shoulder and pointed past him.

Nyle turned. The Jacuzzi was fifteen feet from the back patio, which was shielded from the sun by a slanted terra cotta roof. The space in between housed half a dozen plastic chaise lounges (just the other day Steve and Dom had filmed a massage scene there, Steve giggling and guffawing as he gently, frightfully fiddled with Dom's balls with one hand while holding up a camcorder with the other). Two of the chairs were covered in bugs, four inches long with arched legs, pinprick eyes, green exoskeletons the color of bleached grass.

"Holy shit dude," the producer said. He was standing on the other side of the hot tub, zooming the camera in on Nyle and Bailey, lens focused in on the pulsing bites Bailey was gnarling into Nyle's traps and throat. His name was Jake, and he was the only person Nyle had any contact with from the parent company. Jake had called Nyle with the news he'd been offered a four-week stint in Hottie House based on his application video, a stay that would pay two grand plus food, and that was only the base for a two-show-per-day schedule with other financial benefits available if he went above and beyond that. Jake's voice was a high sing-songy thing, always over-emphasizing the sexiness of the diddling going on in front of the camera. Nyle had trained himself to block out Jake's presence, even when he hovered near, pointing the camera at Nyle's crotch or hitting pause and making what Jake called "an artistic suggestion" about the manner in which Nyle was masturbating.

At first, they tried to ignore the bugs. After taking in the spectacle—the two chaises looked like they were billowing and moving, scutch-green and swirly with motion—Nyle turned around and pressed his mouth to Bailey's shoulder; he tasted like the hot chlorine of the pool, slick and salty, the muscles thick and hard beneath Nyle's lips. Bailey's hands found their way back to Nyle's waist, fingertips grazing his skin under the surface of the water. The script—if one could call something unwritten but plotted out before shooting a script—was for them to kiss and flit and look at one another with their manufactured moony eyes for approximately six minutes before pulling themselves up out of the Jacuzzi. Nyle would then lie on the hot concrete on his back while Bailey rubbed down his thighs and chest then worked at his dick for a few minutes before trading places. They would then move to the chaises (no chance of that now; Jake would come up with some alternative) and lie next to one another, finishing themselves off with a grunted flourish.

But then, as Nyle moved his hands to cup Bailey's ass, the bugs started up: chiseling, stringy noise, louder than that of cicadas and lacking the fluty changing pitch. It sounded to Nyle like the hissing of a shower on full blast. The din was so loud he actually winced. Bailey made a show of covering his ears with his dripping hands.

"Okay, boys," Jake shouted from behind the camera. "Bailey, Brad, I think we're gonna have to relocate."

None of the guys went by their real names; only Jake knew those. To everyone else, Nyle was Brad, a name he chose for its beefy all-Americanness; it evoked Brad Pitt and Bradley Cooper. Nyle didn't know any Brads who weren't one hundred percent straight alpha males who drank heavy American beers and ate cheeseburgers bigger than their fists. It felt strange to respond to the foreign name, to train himself to reply to it. Nyle wondered at the other guys' names, who Bailey and Steve and Dom and Adam really were. Their pseudonyms cast a sheen between them even when their clothes were shed; although they could see and touch and feel one another's bodies, the knowledge that they were holding a bit of themselves back gave each of them a mechanical, robotic sway, their theatricality and falseness amplified as they kissed.

Nyle followed Bailey out of the hot tub but stopped when Bailey did, dripping water onto the cement patio. The bugs had already multiplied, the other chaise lounges covered in sawing green bodies.

"I think they're locusts," Bailey said, turning to Nyle. He shrugged. "I'm a bio major."

This slip of personal information felt like a starburst. Bailey had so far mostly been a grunting, laughing jock, voice a manufactured octave lower than sounded natural, his conversational time spent making jokes about sex and drinking. Nyle had thought him a bit of a caveman in that way, physically appealing but intellectually flavorful as mud. But this spark of educational gusto made Nyle think twice about Bailey but also twice about how the others viewed him. He was a lit major, interested in the prose of Nathaniel Hawthorne and Edgar Allan Poe, details he'd not shared with anyone, even Jake, who had only seen Nyle's carefully-arranged bedroom in his audition tape; he'd hung up a poster depicting a scantily-clad model wrapping herself around a gargantuan Bud Light bottle, swept all of his anthologies and novels from his desk and replaced them with a mess of pens and notebooks.

"Huh," Jake said, standing close to the naked duo, camera lowered to his side. "Let's maybe go around the pool to the other side?"

"They won't attack us," Bailey said over the noise. "Just, you know, be quick."

They scampered past the chaise lounges and through the glass sliding doors that led to the kitchen, where Steve was doing a live shoot, naked while he fried plantains in a cast-iron skillet. Steve was the most muscular guy in the house, incredibly popular, his chat rooms full of goggling fans. As Bailey and Nyle slipped into the kitchen, Steve was laughing and dancing in a circle, waggling his ham-hock butt cheeks toward the webcam on his laptop. The wok in which the plantains fried, sizzled, and spat.

"What up, dudes?" Steve said, saluting toward Nyle and Bailey. He reached out with his free hand—the other held a metal spatula—and swiveled the computer in their direction. Bailey, quick on the pickup, smiled, tongue waggling out, and did a quick crotch thrust toward the camera. Nyle waved and heard Jake duck out of the way. The producer rarely showed himself, and certainly wasn't ever around during live shoots; keeping up the illusion that these weren't paid-for performances was key. The sense that the guys in Hottie House really did care about their viewers, wanted to be slathered over by anonymous watchers with usernames like ChaiHot69 and SpanxDude, was central to the site's success, and seeing a producer would break the magical hold that the hotties in Hottie House held over their fans. And the greater the success, the greater the paychecks. Nyle moved to block Jake's darting body as he army-crawled to the other side of the kitchen island.

"Bro," Bailey said. "Have you seen the shit outside?"

Steve blinked, his visage of suave, muscular masculinity trembling for a second before he leaned in and told his viewers he'd be back in a quick sec.

"What is it?" He craned his neck to look past Nyle. "Oh, fuck."

The swarm had grown into a carpet of green on the cement, writhing as the locusts' legs, angled at forty-five degrees in paired points, sawed. Their song filled the air, overtaking the sound of the popping oil.

Dom swaggered into the kitchen, a cereal bowl in one hand. He wore a pair of mesh shorts that swept down past his knees. His legs were thick with hair; unlike the others, he did not keep them shaved or even crop the hair short (when it was less than half an inch long, the cameras wouldn't pick it up). Every session, Jake had explained, needed at least one jock like Dom to appeal to certain hirsute appetites. Dom's torso featured two thick swirls of body hair, one that covered his chest, the other a wider thatch that spread out in a thicket from his navel like the train on a wedding dress.

With his free hand he scratched at the skin just above the elastic band of his shorts. He yawned.

"What's up with the bugs?" he said. He'd woken only an hour ago, after a late-night naked weightlifting session. His bedroom window, he said, was covered in insects when he woke up. "I thought it was, like, four in the morning or some shit."

"Hey guys," Steve yelled toward the webcam, "we're gonna take this into my room. Gotta save the plantains for later." He shrugged, then looked around the kitchen before leaning back down to the laptop. He winked. "I'm sure we can come up with something else to do with the rest of our time." Steve lifted the computer and exited the kitchen, bare feet slapping on the linoleum.

Jake popped up and set the Canon on the island as soon as Steve was out of earshot. "Well," he said, looking back and forth from Bailey to Nyle. "I guess we should relocate. How about the pool table? We'll do some establishing shots later to explain the location change once those things are gone." He fluttered a hand toward the patio. The bugs now covered the lower half of the sliding doors, clinging like they were suctioned to the glass.

Nyle was happy to escape. The locusts unsettled a puzzle piece in his gut; all the tingling warmth and tightness he'd felt while in the Jacuzzi with Bailey had dissipated, and he marched through their scene on automatic. They took a few shots at the table, feigning a wagering system by which the man who sunk more balls would be serviced by the other; Nyle won, and he leaned back against the table while Bailey plied his torso with kisses as he worked his way down. Normally, Nyle would worry about becoming too excited too quickly, body hot and rigid by the time Bailey was at his crotch, but the thrum of locusts had sucked away all the tormenting sexiness of the moment; as Bailey worked, his saliva and suction and the heat of his breath did nothing for Nyle until he forced himself to focus, hard, on what was happening.

The shoot lasted twenty-five minutes ("Perfect!" Jake said), ending with them both slouched in a pair of leather wing-backed chairs, smiling toward the camera. After Jake stopped filming they each ran to their private bathrooms—each guy had his own bedroom with an en suite—and showered. Nyle turned the water to scalding, scrubbing hard at his chest and stomach, skin scoured pink when he was finished.

The small portcullis-shaped window laid in the grouted tile wall of the shower was covered in bugs, their song erupting while Nyle toweled off, as if rising in a choral judgment of what he had just done and would do again that evening.

Friday nights were saved for group shows, usually something absurd in its sexual exploit; at the end of their first week together, the guys had painted one another's balls like Easter eggs. Tonight Jake produced a pair of Hippity Hops, which they would mount naked and bound around the living room like they were navigating an obstacle course, one at a time, while the others hooted and watched, flexing for Jake's roving camera.

Adam, Dom, and Steve were their usual boisterous selves, laughing and cavorting and offering one another high fives. Steve drank a mimosa from a red plastic cup, pumping his thick bicep as Dom navigated the obstacle course: around the sofa, past the dining room table, narrowly squeaking between two recliners, then across the finish line, a jump rope laid before the television. Nyle, whose amplified shyness was one of his persona's traits ("We have a swath of fans who love the brooding, sensitive type!" Jake had said when he hired Nyle), leaned against the dining room table and watched, bobbing his head in quiet encouragement. But he noticed something was wrong with Bailey, who wouldn't quite look at him. He would clap and smile toward the others, but any time Nyle caught his eye he was sure Bailey glanced away, directing his boyish excitement elsewhere.

After the shoot was over, Dom and Steve, finally dressed in cargo shorts and tank tops, nestled themselves before the TV to play *Call of Duty 4*. Nyle sealed himself up in his bedroom, his roommates' excited howls over headshots and perfect snipes keeping him awake. He lay staring up at the ceiling fan, watching the blades swim through the dark. The locusts covered his window in a heavy blanket so that dots of moonlight shone through like a tiny constellation of stars on the far wall. Their song had been vibrating through the house for so many hours that the noise was nothing to Nyle, an ambient tinnitus that melted into the background. When he did finally swirl into the bracken of sleep, he dreamt of gigantic locusts leaping through a meadow; he and Bailey, naked, were riding atop a pair of them, bounding through chaffs of sharp wheat, their calves scarred by the scratchy grain. Their destination was a swirling purple void on the horizon. Bailey's locust caught one of its legs on a rock and stumbled, sending Bailey crashing, and no matter how Nyle exhorted his locust or pounded his fists on its craggy exoskeleton, the bug would not go back, so Nyle chose to leap off, the sensation of falling from a great height wrenching him from sleep.

Jake slept on a pull-out sofa in one of the villa's unused rooms when he discovered that his car, a smooth white Altima parked near the door, was covered in locusts, as were the front porch and curled driveway. He'd spent hours on his iPhone last night, surfing the news; apparently the bugs were plaguing all of LA. Santa Monica Boulevard, the Decker Canyon Road, Alameda Street: they were all covered in locusts, those that had been squashed by car tires and SUVs replaced by a new, churring flock. Hollywood was in shambles, the sign on Mount Lee a seething mass of vibrating letters.

He gathered the guys together in the living room.

"We can do some indoor shoots," Jake said, "but that's it. I already called one of our tech guys to change the schedule on the website. Adam, your live naked brunch show can still go, but not on the patio. And we'll probably cancel next week's Grillin' Games monthly finale if these bugs aren't gone."

Adam nodded. He was the resident surfer dude, hair shining like sunlight as it bristled against his ears. Adam looked like a former cross-country runner who started downing protein shakes after he turned eighteen: muscular but lean, more sinew than mass, the paired heads of his biceps distinct and twitchy with every movement he made. Counting the threaded fibers of his legs was easy.

"And what if they aren't gone? Isn't our contract up?" Nyle said.

"Some etymologists are working on an eradication plan," Jake said. "So we hope it won't come to that."

"You mean entomologists," Bailey said.

Jake blinked.

"Etymologists study words. Entomologists study bugs." Bailey looked around at the group. "Just wanted to clarify."

"Anyway," Jake said, swatting at his thighs with his hands and standing from his place on the couch. "For now, just relax. The fridge and pantry are stocked, you've got video games and your phones. We'll do Adam's solo at one, then Nyle's, and I think the rest of you have a trio shoot, yeah?"

They nodded then dispersed like tumbles of water, Steve and Dom to work out—without a camera, for once, so they could actually focus on their bench press form—while Adam padded off to take a shower and shave before his show. Nyle blinked toward Bailey, who said nothing and hustled to the kitchen, presumably to make his regular breakfast of four over-easy eggs and three sausage links with buttered wheat toast. Nyle stayed where he was, listening to the ever-present chirrup of the locusts, amplified now that he stood alone.

He came to Hottie House because it seemed like the easiest way to finally hook up with a guy. Yeah, there was the awkwardness of taping himself, fawning a sexy excitement at braying his hands over his chest and stomach and crotch, staring into his webcam knowing that, as soon as he stopped the recording and uploaded it with his profile—which asked for height, weight, penis size, fun facts, sexual history, HIV status, whether he'd popped for any other STIs in the last three years—a stranger would watch, casting judgments on the physical appeal of his body, whether his style of masturbation would be salivating for the Hottie House audience, analyzing the likely profit margin of employing him for a month.

But all of that was somehow simpler. Nyle's college was nestled in a tiny northern Missouri town, and while the school was a liberal oasis in an otherwise thick block of red, he could never shake the sense that sexuality wasn't included in the tiny blue pinprick. And what was worse, he didn't have a clue how to tell if another guy was interested. Girls were easy, and he'd certainly made plenty of inroads there; during his freshman year he'd tossed his virginity away less than a week after settling into his dorm, irking his roommate, who walked in to see Nyle's ass twitching from atop his lofted bed. With girls, the default assumption was that you had a chance. But if you were a guy like Nyle whose eyes flitted over other men's bodies and smiles and gestures while searching for clues that they might be interested in you the way you were interested in them, never quite clear on what those clues actually were, the world became muddy, storm-ridden. The wrong mistake could get you punched in the nose or, with the wrong hypermasc idiot, stabbed. Or worse.

So Hottie House had seemed simple by comparison. Nyle had tamped down the burbling anxiety that smacked him when he first took his pants off with the camera recording. He tossed himself on his bed, spread his legs out, and uncapped a small bottle of generic lube. When his hand curled and made the first stroke he felt a flutter, had to tell himself to look directly at the little pinpoint at the rim of his camera that glowed a dark ruby, a blood red beacon announcing that he was letting the world in.

Jake was wrong. Though a Dr. Adrian Kaiser, a leading entomologist from UC-Berkeley, did drive up to LA to study the locust explosion alongside three other bug experts, they were collectively stumped. Nothing explained the concentrated migration, and none of their solutions— which they refused to share during public interviews—were deemed logistically manageable. Dr. Kaiser, a sandy-haired plank of a person, did admit, squinting into the screen as he stood off to the side of the 405, the shock of bugs behind him like a moving, living putting green, that one proposal had been sent to Washington, D.C., but was rejected by the CDC for its inherent safety issues.

That pronouncement came four days after the arrival of the locusts, and there was no eradication in sight. Because the villa wasn't outfitted with cable, the boys spent hours huddled around streaming news videos on their computers or scanning articles on *Yahoo* and *Buzzfeed* and *Vice*, keeping abreast of updates, which were meager and unhelpful. Bug lovers posted on blogs about the excitement of this strange phenomenon, and ridiculous videos of men and women cavorting toward the locusts became hits on YouTube, their arms and legs covered in wriggling bugs. The thought of all those slippery, prickly legs sawing against Nyle's flesh made him shiver.

Production on shoots halted after seven days, not because any of the guys refused to work, but because Jake wouldn't let them.

"Your contracts are technically up," he said, shrugging. "I can't renegotiate without our legal team signing off on extensions."

"You couldn't just have them email something?" Bailey said.

Jake shrugged. "Site traffic is also down at the moment. Everyone is so focused on the bugs that even porn is in a mini-slump."

"We could do something bug-themed," Bailey offered.

While the others had accepted Jake's moratorium on shoots with shrugs and apathy, Bailey was the singular voice of regret, posing suggestions both believable and absurd, anything to convince the producer to record them again; Nyle half-expected Bailey to blurt out an offer to do a shoot for free, no contract necessary, as if Bailey didn't have a room of his own to go bust a nut in if he was that deprived. The only explanation Nyle could muster was that he had been right when they were lapping at one another in the Jacuzzi: it wasn't about money or fame for Bailey; he wanted to touch and kiss and feel the others, too.

And yet he continued to avoid Nyle. Bailey would joke and socialize with Dom and Adam and Steve, laughing and insulting and high-fiving when a digital comrade-in-arms pulled a solid snipe in *Duty*, but he wouldn't settle his eyes on Nyle for more than a quick moment when Nyle entered a room. If they found themselves alone together, Bailey cleared his throat and mumbled some excuse to escape.

Nyle was running on the treadmill in the basement gym. He huffed it to a compilation of pounding popular seventies and eighties rock, Kansas screeching out "Carry On My Wayward Son" when he heard the scrape of the door: Bailey. Their eyes met. Bailey spun and left the room.

Nyle showered, letting the hot blast of water sluice off the gunky sweat that hardened against his skin like a shell. He took a razor to his torso, careful around his nipples where he plied the shaving cream with extra thickness. Jake had suggested they maintain their regular routines, prepare themselves in case a miracle happened and the locusts disappeared with the same speed they'd appeared; Jake was sure he could maneuver contract extensions for all of them— their ratings, pre-bug, had been among the highest yet, and summer was only halfway over—so they should be ready for shoots at any moment. While Nyle whisked the blade along his stomach he looked at the window, where only the tiniest slivers of natural light popped through the glass so crowded with insect bodies he was almost convinced it would burst, cave in under the weight so the locusts would crowd around him and eat him alive. He reached out one hand and pressed it to the glass, a thin transparent sheath between his fingers and their buzzing bodies. Nyle thought he could feel the tick of their prickled legs, but he decided no, that was just the pulse of his own body, the blood flowing through the tiny capillaries buried just beneath his smoothed skin.

On Monday, a week and a half after the appearance of the locusts and three days after Nyle had expected to fly back to Missouri, he was lying in bed, holding a beaten copy of *Twice-Told Tales*, rereading "Dr. Heidegger's Experiment," his favorite Hawthorne story. His American Romanticism professor had been unabashedly distraught when it was a big fat dud for the class that past spring. Students had stared at one another in their circle of desks, owl-eyed and slack-jawed while their professor leaned forward, slicing a hand through the air palm-up, homilizing on the story's rich plot and psychological insights into the human desire for youth, life, and eternal beauty. Nyle had been dazzled, and during that robust lecture had decided he wanted to sit amongst young English majors for the rest of their lives and explain to them the riches of literature.

Dr. Heidegger's friends were on the cusp of drinking the water when a knock, so soft Nyle thought he might have imagined it, came at his door. He shoved the book into the drawer of his nightstand and called out to whoever was on the other side, knowing, somehow, that it was Bailey.

He stood in a wife beater and a pair of black boxer briefs suctioned against his thighs to show off the striations of his quadriceps.

"Yeah?" Nyle said, swallowing.

The point of Bailey's Adam's apple bobbled like a fishing lure. He cleared his throat. "Can I come in?"

Something in Bailey's voice made Nyle sit up. A hitch, a catch, wobbling and seductive at the same time. He nodded. Bailey shut the door without asking, the wood thudding heavily in the frame. He sat on the end of the mattress, which wheedled and squeaked under the thickness of his body. Nyle moved his feet, bare legs pointed away from Bailey.

"These bugs are crazy," Bailey said, staring down at his hands.

"Yeah."

"You think we'll ever get out of here?"

"Eventually, I guess."

"You worried?"

Nyle sat up straight. "Are you?"

Bailey shrugged. "I don't know." He looked straight at Nyle, who hadn't before noticed the shocking violent color of Bailey's eyes: an unnatural green, glowing like something biohazardous, radioactive.

"You've been acting weird," Nyle said. He cleared his throat. "Ever since the bugs came."

Bailey's gaze returned to his lap. Nyle could see, through the tight outline of the boxer briefs, that Bailey had an erection. He felt a glazing warmth bloom in his mouth as if his teeth and cheeks were being covered in the copper of his own blood. Nyle grinded his teeth, flexed his jaw, and said nothing. Neither did Bailey, and the sound of the locusts coated them both in its lazy slalom of noise.

"Sorry," Bailey said finally, the sound cracking through the room. He leaned back, falling against the mattress. Nyle barely moved his feet out of the way before they were crushed under Bailey's bulk. "I'm just. I don't know."

He stared at the ceiling, body stretched so the fabric of his shirt rode up. The erection had subsided, if the coiled mass of fabric at his crotch was any indication. "You ever think you know something about yourself and then think you might be wrong?"

Nyle exhaled, a sharp punchy sound. "Yeah, I guess so."

Bailey turned on his side, head anchored by his bent arm. "Really?"

"Yes."

"Hmm."

"What?"

"Nothing." Another silence wrapped itself around them, the coo of the bugs rising in the background. Finally, Bailey started sidling up the bed so he was parallel with Nyle. "Could I, you know, uh."

"What?" Nyle said, trying to hide the feeling overcoming his lungs, a tightness like balled fists were squeezing his ribcage from all sides.

"Could I just stay here?"

"What?"

"Sleep here. Just sleep, I mean. Not, you know, euphemistically."

"Oh."

"We don't really get to just be in this place, do we?"

Nyle nodded.

"Thanks," Bailey said.

Nyle reached up and turned off the bedside light.

Nyle woke filmed in sweat. The heat trapped beneath the sheets had turned the bed into an oven, and the room smelled vaguely like a locker room.

He noticed two things immediately: first, Bailey was gone.

Second, the house was silent. Not just silent. Something deeper, animate in its quiet.

Then he noticed more: sunlight was streaming through his window, a thick bar of white shine. The bugs weren't singing, because the bugs were gone.

And even though Bailey was gone, his clothing was not, his boxer briefs and t-shirt pooled on the floor like flagstones leading toward the bedroom door, which yawned open into the hall, where creamy light from the living room streamed like custard.

Nyle leapt from bed and half-walked, half-ran out the bedroom, down the hall, toward the living room. Steve, Dom, and Adam—and Jake, ever-present, pestilential Jake— were nowhere to be found. The ticking silence of morning thrummed in Nyle's ears as he reached the front door of the villa, which, like all the other doors leading to the outside world, had been shut for ten days. Now it stood open, letting in the sharp dewy smell of morning, the inviting fresh breeze of the far-off ocean and the wafting sounds of bristling tree branches as they swayed in the wind. Nyle paused, long enough for his nostrils to take in the freshness pulsing into the house. He shut his eyes.

Then he approached the front door. The warmth of the still-rising sun chattered on his thighs but, he felt the chill of shock press into his fingers and toes and wriggle inward.

Bailey stood on the villa's weedy front lawn. He was naked, staring up toward the sky. A cloud of locusts hovered above him, twenty feet in the air, a whirling green thicket of plague. They buzzed and hummed, their collective voice throbbing.

Nyle called out. Bailey turned to look at him and raised his arms out wide, extended like a priest enjoining his congregation to pray.

Nyle saw sadness in Bailey's eyes, and knowledge that their one night was liminal, temporary. Like the bugs, it came from nowhere and would vanish away into the atmosphere. It had nothing to do with sex or orgasm, had been a gateway to a hungered-for closeness, to the thump and thrum of blood, the bristle of hair and skin and breath. Things they could reach for and rake their fingers through but not quite hold.

"My name," Bailey said, looking at Nyle, blond body hair glimmering in the sun.

Before he could say more, the locusts, as if on cue, started their descent.

Nyle released his grip on the door frame and sprung, catapulting himself into the yard, breaking free, saying no, trying to let go and take hold at the same time.

Demon Lover

Micah discovered his boyfriend was a demon when Lucas made the sun disappear for three days. The darkness was a nice break, an excuse for them to ignore the stacks of freshman comp papers they both needed to grade, to skip out on their graduate seminars, to put off marking up the forty-page vampire erotica one of the women in their fiction workshop submitted the week before. Classes were cancelled, not just because of the sun's spooky vanishing but because Lafayette was getting the leftovers from Tropical Storm Nina, rain pounding down onto windows and car windshields, swirling into overflowing storm drains in the center of dipped parking lots. Before Lucas caused the darkness, the electricity had snapped off with a sad sigh, the mid-morning news blipping off the television, the pebbled refrigerator dropped its eternal low growl and the reading lamp that had been the bedroom's only illumination curled away its light like a precious secret.

They were in bed when Lucas confessed. He pressed a hand against Micah's navel.

"I need to tell you something," he said.

"What?"

"The lumps on my head, the ones I said were sebaceous cysts?" Lucas craned his neck to look at Micah. "You know, here?"

"Yeah? What about them?" Micah's forehead was sooted with sweat; even rainy Louisiana was still Louisiana, still October, and still hot, especially with the air conditioning not working.

"They're not cysts. They're horns."

"Horns?"

"Yeah." Lucas leaned away. "There's some stuff you should know."

They showered, feeling their way into the bathroom and finding the knobs, adjusting the water to slightly less than scalding. Micah scrubbed Lucas's back and crotch, then Lucas did the same for Micah. They had slept together for the first time after a meet and greet at the home of the director of the creative writing program, and had hardly spent a day not naked together since. Micah had arrived at the party late, getting lost on Johnston Street trying to find the appropriate turnoff, and by the time he arrived Lucas was blitzed, a half-empty bottle of expensive Beaujolais in one hand, an Abita in the other. He was a year older than Micah and the most accomplished writer in the program even though he was headed into only his second year, so the faculty and other students laughed off his alcohol problem. Plus, he handled his booze pretty well, becoming gregarious and hilarious once enough of it had tickled his bloodstream. It made his cheeks flush a lilac color that swirled along his skin as if painted by a steady, careful hand. He and Micah had got to talking, discovering that they lived in the same apartment complex. Micah, who only drank two beers that night, offered Lucas a ride home. Lucas stumbled into Micah's apartment instead of his own and must have read something in Micah's eyes because when he was offered a glass of water, he set it aside and instead kissed Micah on the lips. Then he marched into Micah's bedroom and passed out.

They tried the next morning, rubbing at one another's testicles and pressing fingers along their perinea. But when both were naked and ready to go, Lucas moaned and rubbed his temples.

"I think I'm too hungover for this. Brunch instead?" They made out for a few minutes, breath hot and spiced with Purple Haze and grappa, then agreed that crab cake eggs benedict at the Blue Dog would cure Lucas's headache. Micah drank too many bottomless mimosas, and later, the only thing he could remember was Lucas asking him what he wrote. Micah, taking a deep sip from his champagne glass, said, "Bisexual fantasy. You?" and Lucas, blue eyes wet and dreamy, responded, "Erotic male-male poetry, with the periodic foray into fiction."

And that was that.

They toweled off and sat in the dark living room, Micah peeping through the slats of the vertical blinds. His cell phone said midday, but the lot was crushed by darkness deep as midnight. Lucas toted a box of Cheez-Its from the pantry and curled up cross-legged next to him. The only light came from their phone screens, cascading them in techno-wiz blue and white.

"So when you said horns."

"Yeah." Lucas set down the box and reached both hands up to his head, curling them in circular fashion against his scalp to swirl his blond hair, which he kept short so it edged toward translucent. Micah waved his phone over Lucas's head. There, just above the hairline, were the two bumps. "These guys. They're horns."

"Horns."

"I have unusual parentage."

"Uh huh."

Lucas grabbed at Micah's hand, rubbing the back of his knuckles like he was stoking firewood. "But that doesn't change anything."

"Okay."

"But there's something else."

"There's something else."

Lucas released Micah's hand and knocked on the window. "The funky dark? I think I might have done that."

"Might. Have done that."

"The truth is," Lucas said with a sigh, his lean chest and shoulders curling inward, "I think I'm going through puberty."

Lucas, it turned out, was over two hundred years old, born just after the start of the War of 1812.

"But born isn't the right word. It's hard to explain. My mother was a succubus, and they do this whole eggs and fire thing and a ritual to give birth. There's no vaginal stretching or anything."

"I went through puberty when I was thirteen. Shouldn't you be over it by now? Your voice isn't even breaking."

"Demon years," Lucas said, fluttering a dismissive hand. "Anyway. You know how teenage boys get uncontrollable erections and all that?" He pointed out the window.

"Causing darkness is like your version of a nocturnal emission, then?"

Lucas shrugged. "I guess so."

"But you look so, um."

"You can say it."

"Normal."

"Turns out my human genes are the stronger ones. Dad was a French soldier."

"You're French?"

"*Oui, oui.* But that's all I know. Was raised by Mom."

"Where?"

"We hid out in Boston."

"Not, like, hell?"

"She wasn't interested in mischief or torment."

"So she was, like, a reformed, good-spirited succubus?"

"I suppose so."

"So what went wrong with you?"

Lucas swooped in and bit at Micah's earlobe.

The power snapped on in the middle of the night, a sudden sizzle of noise, the television blurbing back to life so Anderson Cooper's voice shouted from the living room. The reading lamp blitzed at Micah's eyes like a heat lamp over limp french fries.

Micah jolted awake, but Lucas, a deep sleeper, didn't stir, his tiny snoring noises swallowed up by the electronica in the living room. Micah slithered out of bed and shut things down. He paused in the living room and looked out into the grim dark: the sodium lights along the parking lot had returned to life. They seemed weaker than usual, less powerful in the tar-thick black that Lucas had swept into town, but maybe that was an effect of the rain still seething against the window.

When he slipped back into bed, Micah ran a finger lightly over each of Lucas's horns. They were malleable, like little clusters of fat under his fingers. He'd expected nuggets of tree bark, like calluses. Lucas murmured in his sleep and

Micah pulled his hand back, then curled himself up next to the sleeping body that gave off an immense, solid heat.

"This doesn't really make sense." The second day of darkness passed, finally catching attention nationally, Jake Tapper looking puzzled on CNN, local newscasters exaggerating their confusion with bulging eyes as they reported through the gloom, standing in front of the Cajundome or City Hall or Evangeline Downs racetrack. The darkness hovered mostly over Lafayette, petering further out, Alexandria suffering a perpetual duskiness, Baton Rouge getting a few hours of dawnish light, New Orleans gloomy but sunlit.

"Of course it doesn't," Lucas said, plopping down on the couch, a heated frozen burrito perched on a plate in his lap.

"No, not the darkness. You. You're two hundred and only going to graduate school now?"

"You think this is my first rodeo?"

"Huh?"

"I have a doctorate in chemistry, one in anthropology, and one in economics."

"What? Really?"

"I mean, I don't go boasting about it. I didn't even send in my transcripts from my last program. I have all the regalia in my closet, though."

Micah felt woozy.

"But you look so—"

"Young and fresh and unmolested by years of writing dissertations? Why thank you. I do take care of my skin."

"So that accounts for what, fifteen years?"

"I also worked at Macy's, but that was when it was called Famous-Barr." He took a bite out of his burrito and then spit it out. "Ack. Too hot. I think I burned my tongue."

"Do you know when this will stop?" Micah said, rapping on the window.

Lucas shrugged. "Sooner or later. Aren't you enjoying our time off?" He pressed a hand at Micah's crotch. "It's not like I can't think of ways to pass the time."

Micah swatted at his groping hand. "Stop that."

They watched television. Classes were still cancelled, emails coming in every few hours pushing back the time and date that the university would reopen. They had at least forty-eight more before they would have to read the mammoth vampire erotica with its run-on sentences, adverb-filled sex scenes, and four-line descriptions of cum shots.

That night, Micah slipped into bed and felt Lucas reach between his legs. He grunted and shifted aside.

"What's this about?"

"I'm still processing."

"I'm still me."

"Are you sure? Is there anything else I should know about?"

"I'm HIV negative. I get tested regularly."

Micah switched on the reading light and tossed back the sheets. Lucas slept in the nude, and his body was on full display, milky in the harsh LED bulb.

"Look me over, then," Lucas said, spinning onto his stomach. "No tail." He flexed his triceps and pulled back his shoulder blades while he wiggled his ass. "No wings or weird elbow claws." He sat up. "I don't have gross nails. You've seen my bathroom. I keep emery boards by my toothbrush."

Micah poked and prodded. He ran a hand along Lucas's left butt cheek, wheedled at the chapped skin of his elbow, flicked at his shoulder blade.

"See?"

"Still."

"It's not like we're going to make little half-demon babies."

"Wouldn't they be quarter-demon babies? You had a human dad."

"I study iambic pentameter, not genetics." Lucas pressed Micah to the bed and kissed him on the mouth, his breath mouthwash minty. "That's one I haven't gotten to yet."

"Will you always look like this?" Micah said, pressing a hand to Lucas's cheek.

"I look how I want to look."

"And will that ever change?"

"I'm sure it will," Lucas said, kissing Micah's hand. At least his breath wasn't sulfur and brimstone.

The next day, they sat on the couch with their copies of the vampire erotica.

"I can't believe there are forty pages of this shit," Lucas said, gnawing on a red pen. "There are adverbs in every other sentence."

"And it's titled 'Rigor Whortus.' How did she get into this program?"

"Apparently she's an excellent theorist. She's just taking the fiction workshop for the hell of it."

"It's certainly hell-like."

"Oh please," Lucas said, scribbling a note in a margin. "That is not how vampires dressed in the early nineteen hundreds." He looked up. "Don't worry. There were only, like, four of them left at the time. I'm sure they've been either staked by now or toasted by the sun."

Micah rolled his eyes toward the dark outdoors. It was one-fifteen in the afternoon and looked like midnight. The drunk frat boys who lived across the parking lot should have been stumbling around, a two-story beer bong waggling from the upper-story balcony. Instead, outside was silent.

"I can't take more of this," Lucas said, tossing the manuscript on the coffee table. He spat out his pen and turned to Micah. "Tell me a secret."

"What?"

"It only feels fair. I showed you mine." He plumbed his horns with his thumbs. "How's it go? You show me yours."

"But you already know my secrets," Micah said. "I told you about the time I peed myself in seventh grade. I even told you about when I got that poorly-timed boner in the locker room after basketball practice and Slade Malcolm yanked my towel off."

"Those are just embarrassing stories." Lucas leaned closer. "I mean something you've never shared with anyone."

"You've never told anyone else you're a demon?"

"Nope. You are the first."

"I feel like this is a line you've used before."

Lucas gripped Micah's hand and tilted his head forward, chin disappearing against his chest. "I'm serious. Never have. You're the first. I promise."

"Why tell me all this in the first place?"

"Why do you think?"

Micah felt little edges cracking in his bones. "Okay. Fine." Sweat clung at the sides of his nose. "You're the first man I've ever been with."

"That's it?"

"No, I mean at all. I'd never even kissed another guy before."

"Oh." Lucas froze, then seemed shaken by a pair of invisible hands. He pulled Micah to him, clinging tight. "Oh."

When Lucas fell asleep, body slick with the warm and sour sweat of sex, Micah flicked on the bedside lamp and looked him over. Lean, sinewy shoulders like conch shells, pecs the size of saucer plates, nipples dark like pennies. His hips were slanted and bony, the skin of his abdomen smooth and hairless, but his legs were shagged with blond curls, like he was a sun-bleached satyr. His breathing was wheezy and regular, the air wet and sweet like a menthol lozenge.

Micah turned off the light and slipped out of bed. He unlocked the apartment door, swinging it open slowly so it didn't croak out. The pebbled concrete was rough on his feet, the air cool with the rain that had blustered away, leaving behind a crispness that smelled faintly of salt and boiled shrimp.

He stepped into the darkness. It felt alive, a thick mucus that seeped against his skin like slime. Micah wanted to pull back, shear at his arms like bugs were crawling along his flesh, but he resisted the tingling urge and inhaled, feeling the foggy black dig into his lungs, pour into his stomach. He held his breath, let the black echo and murmur there, fighting its way into his liver, his kidneys, his ribs. He held on for so long that he felt the push in his eyeballs, the faded blue light of the streetlamps spangling like sparklers.

He doesn't know it yet, but in the morning the sun will rise, the darkness Lucas has spewed out retreating into the sky. Lucas will fix breakfast, frying potatoes and sausage links and sprinkling the pan with Monterey cheese. He will bring breakfast into bed and kiss Micah deeply and tell him that the vampire erotica is actually pretty good.

"What happens in the end?" Micah will ask.

"The vampire will live happily ever after."

"And his human lover?"

"Him too."

They will kiss, then discard their breakfast and kiss some more, their knees knocking together.

But standing in the cool dark, Micah exhaled, feeling the blackness seep away in a long, cold stretch, while the night ticked away. He snuck back inside and shut the door, looking out the window as he passed through the living room toward his sleeping demon lover, the moon obscured by the preternatural dark.

In Memoriam

The summer after I turned sixteen, boys in my subdivision started dying.

First was eighteen-year-old Pauly Dunphy, who had shoulders like a pair of knotted fists and lifeguarded at the community pool where I swam laps and glanced at him through my tinted goggles. He died of congestive heart failure from an undetected weak wall in one of his ventricles. His mother found him cold and twisted in his soiled bedsheets. I went to the funeral and sat near the back, choked by the Windsor knot my father had tied too tight, wondering why the world had cruelly let me fall in love with someone who would die so young.

Tommy De Luca ran into a bees' nest and died of anaphylactic shock from an allergy no one knew about. Sam Elmendorfer electrocuted himself in a freak accident involving a kiddie pool and a boom box, and Peter Santos, who played outfield with me in little league during fourth and fifth grade, was the first of three to be killed in car accidents, while Michael Winters and Beau Sandborne died from alcohol poisoning two weekends in a row.

They were all the eldest, the first-born sons.

So was I.

My mother chewed her lip. My father took a long gulp of skim milk. My twin sister Jenny laid her hand on mine. Her skin was cold even though she was deeply tanned from laying on our back deck. My parents were both teachers, so they were at home most of the summer. They sat quietly together, watching the movies they didn't have time to binge watch during the school year.

"I'm sure you'll be okay," my mother said.

My father nodded.

But then, in June, word got around that our next-door neighbors' son, in his forties, died in a boating accident. He lived in Florida; his younger sister lived with their parents, taking care of her homebound father. I helped her haul twenty-five-pound bags of potting soil from their garage into the back yard sometimes. They had a pool, above-ground, but Jenny and I were never invited over to swim. We didn't go to that funeral.

The couple across the street lost one of their newborn twins—the one who'd been born only sixteen minutes before the other—to SIDS. Two more car accidents claimed the lives of two thirteen-year-olds.

"Seriously," I said one Sunday afternoon. "Have none of you read the Bible?"

My mother shook her head. My father opened a beer and suggested we go for ice cream later. He was bald and bearded and looked like a fuzzy egg.

July brought more deaths: little Gary Harper, only five years old, stood too close to an M-80 firecracker. Cameron Riggs drowned in the neighborhood lake during a late-night skinny-dipping foray gone wrong. A nine-year-old caught pneumonia and never left the hospital.

I became a hermit. No more riding my bike; I didn't want to get squashed by a Ford F-150. No swimming at the pool after Pauly died; I didn't trust the yawning lifeguards with their heavy tans and smooth legs, and I had read about bacteria that could slip right down your throat if some infant shat itself and the chemicals in the water weren't strong enough. My parents wanted to take us to Disney World, and I said I wouldn't go because I knew the plane would crash. They begged and pleaded. I couldn't sleep. The only one who seemed to sympathize was Jenny, who brought me lunch and dinner on an old metal tray she found in the attic when I refused to leave my room. She blinked at me and tried to offer me hugs, but I was worried she might have dragged in ticks from the back yard that would give me Lyme Disease, so I shook my head no.

She helped me track the deaths. We googled our neighborhood and drew up a map on four sheets of paper we taped together. I hung it on my wall. Marking off houses with red seemed too morbid, so I slashed a green X over every house where a boy had died. Jenny stared at it, saying *hmmm* and tapping her cheek with her index finger. Her summer-blonde hair swayed in a tight ponytail while her smart eyes scanned the map. After a minute, she shook her head. She, too, failed to find any pattern predicting where death would strike next; the X's were scattered about the curves and cul-de-sacs like jacks tossed willy-nilly on a carpet.

"Maybe we could slather the front door with cow blood to protect you, like in Exodus."

"Mom would never go for that. And I think it was lamb's blood."

"What if you converted to Judaism?"

"They were Israelites, not Jewish."

"I'm just saying," she said, pointing at the map. "Nick Abrahamson and David Gasko are still alive."

"Maybe I'll read the Torah. Not like I'm going anywhere."

Jenny placed a hand on my shoulder, her touch light and wispy. "I'm just trying to help."

I nodded.

"Are you okay?"

"I'm going to die, Jenny."

"Maybe not."

"But look at the map." By now, half the houses were smeared with green. Months prior, the homeowner's association had paid to print off a subdivision directory, so everyone could know everyone else. I had skimmed through it, sorting out who did and didn't have boys; the latter I colored in yellow. That left maybe ten unblemished.

"Okay," Jenny said. "But there's something else, right?"

"What?"

She removed her hand and turned so we faced each other. She had our father's bad eyes, her own magnified behind cat-eye glasses. She blinked.

"You were friends with Peter."

"A long time ago."

"Still. And what about Pauly?"

An icy claw gouged my belly button. "What about him?"

Jenny rolled her eyes. "Come on. I heard you the night of his funeral."

"I don't know what you're talking about."

"You were crying, Brian. I could hear you." She rapped on the wall above my bed. Her room was on the other side. "We have thin walls." Jenny thumped her hand on my shoulder again. "It's okay. I won't tell anyone." She turned and, before interring me in the tomb of my room, smiled. "It's impossible enough to keep a secret in this house."

The day Anthony Peregrino, a pasty nerd who played Magic: The Gathering and never went outside, was mauled by a bear that trooped through the half-acre of woods behind his house and attacked him while he lit his parents' charcoal grill, I stepped in front of the television where my parents were watching *America's Got Talent*, turned the set off, and stared at them.

"Hey," my dad said, a little whine in his voice. "I wanted to see if Simon was going to hit the golden buzzer."

My mother looked ready to cry.

"Do you just not care?" I said.

They looked at each other, something invisible snaking between them. I saw Jenny perched on the stairs to the second floor, body folded like a chair. Her kneecaps were roughened and dark.

"We're just confident," my father said.

"Confident I'm going to die!"

"No, son. Confident that you're not."

A little peep of a sob escaped my mother. Her blond hair was wavy, face sharp angles like knives. She brushed at her throat with her hand.

"What is going on?" I said.

My father looked at my mother and leaned over to whisper something behind his cupped hand. She shook her head and started crying.

"Please," I croaked "Just yesterday, Mike Robson got sun poisoning and died from shock. It wasn't even sunny. There are only eight houses left."

"We promised one another," my mother said, ignoring me. "We said no matter what." "Promised what?" I said.

My father sighed. "He's going crazy, Danielle."

"Fine," she said. "See if I trust you again. But you'll have to be the one to show him."

"Show me what?"

My father stood and beckoned me to follow. We walked up the stairs. Jenny had scuttled back to her room, but she joined when we passed her door. The attic was accessed at the end of the upstairs hall by a Louisville Everest ladder stuffed up in a stealth panel. My father tugged on its dangly string, dragging the steel ladder out. He climbed up, then I followed and so did Jenny.

The attic was musty, filled with old photo albums, Christmas decorations, our baby toys. A diaper table and small bureau sat in one corner; I had no idea how either had gotten hauled up there. Pink Foamular sagged from between the studs and the air was sticky. I started to sweat, sure I would die of heat exhaustion.

"Come here," our father said, beckoning us to the bureau. It was nestled beneath a porthole window that drew in the sharp evening light, a blur of pinkish yellow that beamed against our father's blank, wide forehead.

Dad bent down, knees popping as he squatted. He pulled open the lowest drawer of the bureau. It coughed out dust, the smell of the past spinning into the hot attic. He rummaged through a scattered heap of folders, printouts, old report cards. He withdrew a trio of photos.

"Here," he said.

The first photo: him and Mom, twenty years ago. Mom's hair was feathered, and Dad wore purple-lensed sunglasses. Between them, an infant boy.

"Who is this?" I said. I could feel Jenny hovering over my shoulder like a pesky wraith.

My father didn't answer.

The second photo was just the boy, a shot looking down into a yellow bassinet. Red glasses were slumped low on his nose, his fingers curled in tiny fists. Arms splayed up at scalene angles, body wrapped in a blue-and-red onesie. I couldn't quite tell what, but something was off about his eyes, slightly unfocused. His head was almost bulbous.

In the final photograph, he was lying in a hospital bed, a cannula tucked in his parchment-thin nostrils.

"Dad," I said, holding out the photos. "Who is he?"

He sighed and tweaked at his nose, pushing his glasses up. "That's Thomas. Your older brother."

They sat us down in the kitchen, my mother pulling a pitcher of lemonade from the fridge, the yellow liquid bobbing with sliced lemons and ice cubes. She kept tizzying around, plucking napkins from the counter, pulling glasses from a cabinet. My father cleared his throat and she sat down.

Thomas had been born with Rett Syndrome, a rare genetic disorder, almost unheard of in boys. Though it could be inherited, neither of my parents were carriers. As with most children who suffered from Rett, Thomas had simply been struck by random, horrendous luck.

"He died when he was thirteen months old," Dad said.

Mom drank her lemonade. When she was done, she refilled her glass and wiped her mouth with the back of her hand.

"It killed us," he said, then winced at his word choice. "It felt impossible to move on."

"Unless," Mom finally said, voice croaky as if she hadn't spoken in months, "we made ourselves forget."

"God," Jenny said, slumping in her seat. She fiddled with the beads of condensation melting into the wood around her glass.

"Then you two came along," Dad said, looking at me. "You were perfect. Healthy." He shifted his gaze to Jenny, peering over his glasses. "Both of you."

The room rang with silence. Our mother sniffed. Her eyes were veined and red.

I exhaled.

Jenny crossed her arms, uncrossed them. Rubbed at her eyeballs.

"So you'll be okay," our mother said.

I looked down at my lap and nodded. We dispersed without another word, Jenny and me to our rooms, Mom and Dad to the living room. We were like a dense fog loosening.

The beginning of August brought the last of the deaths, and I marked each one with my green pen. I skimmed the internet, watched the news. I wanted to know whenever another boy was gone.

My parents changed. At breakfast—I had paroled myself from imprisonment—my mother spoke nonstop about Thomas, his chestnut eyes, his babbling-brook laugh. My father stood behind her and squeezed her shoulders as she remembered, and between bites of French toast she would reach up and place her hand over his. She was glossy with tears all the time, but I sensed a shocked joy in them.

Marty Steinem died of a drug overdose. Jose Figueroa, a state champion cross-country runner, was hit by a car on a backroad during an afternoon jog. Mike Fine ate listeria-ridden lettuce. Each time, I sliced through a house with a green X.

My mother called her sister in Ithaca and had her ship a photo album. Pictures of Thomas appeared on the living room wall. Jenny took one from the attic and set it on a side table in a gilt frame. At meals, we plied our parents for information about our brother, his favorite foods—peas and mashed carrots—and whether he'd ever learned to crawl or babble.

I wondered if the last handful of families were keeping track of the deaths. If the boys in those homes—Taylor Warner, John Fitzel, Andy Weber, Nicholas Peuter—were terrorized by nightmares, the knowledge that their dooms were coming. I wanted to go to them, hug them, squeeze them, tell them goodbye even though I did not know them.

Taylor Warner's parents sent him to a mental institute to keep him safe in a rubber-walled room. The van taking him there crashed, its brakes failing on the interstate. Nicholas Peuter committed suicide one night to get it over with, shooting himself in the head with his father's Glock. John Fitzel's house burned down with him in it when a crockpot malfunctioned. Andy Weber disappeared. His parents lamented his vanishing, his friends wondered *why why why* in interviews. But I understood, and I realized that no one else in the world could know the exact kind of fear every eldest boy in the neighborhood experienced that summer, a gluey nausea gumming between lungs and ribs.

I marked the Weber house even though Andy wasn't confirmed dead; I just knew. I stared at the map. So many green slashes. But something was wrong.

Jenny knocked on the door and came into the room. She hugged me from behind.

"It's over," she said. "For better or worse, I guess."

"Yeah, but."

"But what?"

"I don't know." I waved at the map. "Something's not right."

She cocked her head at me. "You're still here and you thought you wouldn't be. Maybe that's it?"

I shook my head. "Not quite. Maybe? I don't know."

"Maybe we'll never know. Why it happened, I mean." She looked at my map. "Ah," she said. "But I see." She stepped up to the wall and tapped right on our house.

A white blank square amongst so many marked.

"We're no different," Jenny said.

"You're right."

After I drew the green X, Jenny and I stared at the map for a while before I plucked it down, tape dragging away a layer of paint. I folded it and we left the room. As we crossed the living room our parents looked up from the couch. In the yard, I tore the map apart and gave half to Jenny. Without a word we yanked away one house after another. Our parents stepped onto the porch, staring at us. When the map was nothing but confetti, I held my breath, cupped my hands, and heaved the pile into the sky.

The Flood

After their kids flew the coop, Cindy and Wim opened their home to graduate students from the local English department. It was Cindy's idea; Wim just grunted and nodded, not taking the time to wonder why Cindy would be so desperate to refill their home. She was the one who could stand neither clutter nor empty space, holding a garage sale every year to rid the house of anything that human hands had not touched in the last twelve months. This was how they split with nearly half of their wedding gifts, including all of the good china from Cindy's great aunt and the salad spinner given by Wim's cousin Bill. Cindy was immune to her children's desperate wailings when they suddenly developed attachment to the Barbie dolls and Bop Its that sat in the toy room, forgotten until Cindy appeared with her white laundry basket and began declaring items up for deportation. Out goes the dusty Game Boy Advance! Goodbye, Puppy Surprise! But she was also the one to insist on splurging every Christmas, filling not just the tree skirt but the surrounding radius, several times even having to lay out excess spillage on the nearby sofa.

What Wim didn't know about was the dreams. A week's worth of them, so potent and vivid that Cindy woke up out of breath and dizzy, so much sweat sopped into her pillow and the sheets that she stripped the bed every day, running the salty, crusted set through the washer and dryer. In the dreams, which were really just one dream on repeat, her house was filled to bursting with twenty- and thirty-somethings, all graduate students, two of each sort: two poets, two fiction writers, two essayists, two linguists, two Americanists, two folklorists, even two Spenser scholars, who were sharing the couch in the basement and crooning about the House of Pride. Outside, rain was pounding and gushing, drowning the front and back yard and sending cars and SUVs spinning down the street like graceful ballerinas in pirouette. Right before she woke, a voice she could identify as nothing but that of God boomed: *Take them in.*

Cindy was not religious, but the thumping of her heart and the recurrence of her dreams drove her to call up the English department chair, a balding, portly linguist from Georgia whose drinking problem became famous when, after the faculty-student meet and greet two years prior, he drunkenly drove his car through his own bay window and had to take a semester's leave of absence. He transferred Cindy to the graduate coordinator, a Romanian woman who taught seminars on Paul Auster, drama writing, and creative writing pedagogy (claiming, on the first day of said course, that such pedagogy didn't really exist, but then required her students to read everything by Wallace Stegner anyway). They intended to offer housing to four students, Cindy said. The Romanian had a pinched voice that rose at the end of every sentence so Cindy couldn't tell when she was being asked a question, but eventually she hammered out that the woman would send an email with details and Cindy and Wim's contact info to the graduate listserv first thing the next day.

The inquiries came in a tsunami, especially because of the barely-existent rent: they'd asked for a share in the utilities, a willingness to help cook and wash dishes, and one hundred dollars a month, mostly to cover groceries; in return, each student would get a room, but would share one of the two hall bathrooms, both equipped with shower and double marbled vanity. Cindy wanted to just accept the first four applicants—that, to her, seemed the fairest way—but Wim, who had printed out all forty-plus letters of interest, smashed his finger on the stack.

"We can't just take in anyone, Cindy. They could be drug addicts or sexual predators. We need background checks!"

"I highly doubt the university would accept sexual predators into their program."

Wim grunted and crossed his arms. He'd started to look a little bit like a toad since the kids left. His lips protruded, his eyes seeming to slide to the sides of his face, the hunching posture of his rounded shoulders becoming more noticeable daily. Thankfully, his black hair hadn't gone to gray or thinned, and he still coifed it in a pleasant, youthful cut, about two inches long and swooping forward with an upswing at the tips so he resembled an out-of-work boy band member.

"They're writers, Cindy!" he said. "They know how to make themselves look good on paper. We need to interview them."

She sighed, sipped on her glass of Sauvignon Blanc—she'd taken to drinking one glass of wine per night ever since Winnie finally moved out, dismissing Wim's concerned looks by citing studies indicating a glass of wine (never mind that it was supposed to be red) could have the same health benefits as an hour at the gym—and told him fine, if that's what he wanted. But he would be in charge of the show, not her. All she asked was that he get to it quickly, as she wanted the house filled before the fall semester started. She said nothing of the dreams, which had grown and expanded after she made the phone call: now, after the voice made its demands, the house suddenly detached itself from its foundation and started shifting, twisting through the flood of water like the seats on one of those Scrambler rides at amusement parks that jogged one's stomach from left to right and down and up.

Wim made a spreadsheet, staring at Microsoft Excel on the laptop Cindy bought him for his birthday to replace the clunky desktop that took fifteen minutes to warm up and another ten to connect to the internet because he'd laden it with so much excessive software, anti-virus protection and stock tickers and weather apps. At first Wim had refused to use the laptop, but Cindy, in a bit of electronic espionage, changed the log-in password on the old desktop and managed to convince him that the thing had finally lost its gourd.

Cindy allowed Wim's selection process to last exactly two interviews. During the first, Wim answered the door to Jeremy, a tall, slender young man in thick black glasses who looked like he could have been a skinnier Clark Kent. A runner, perhaps someone who went to the gym periodically but mostly to play basketball and huff out pushups. He offered his hand and Wim took it, nodding and inviting him in while Cindy listened as he led the boy into the office off the front door.

"Why do you want to live here?" she heard Wim say.

Jeremy's answer seemed more than acceptable: he was fortunate to be on a fellowship at the university, but that didn't mean he made enough to afford the rent he'd paid last year, over eight hundred dollars a month in an apartment he'd rented blind, moving from St. Louis, Missouri, to Louisiana without ever looking at the place. He was barely able to feed himself, and the drop in rent more than made up for the other chores.

"Chores? That's what you'd call them?"

Cindy tried to stop herself from barging in and ending the interview. She heard the snarl in Wim's voice and could imagine the look on his face. Even though the boy was right—what else *would* you call scrubbing dishes and helping cook meals?—Wim would hate to have tasks described as such. Chores were for children; adults helped one another out, did their *duty*.

She didn't hear Jeremy's response because Wim talked over it, moving on to his next question: "Do you have a criminal record of any kind? And let me remind you we'll be running a background check if you're considered a finalist."

Okay, Cindy thought.

She demanded she sit in on the second interview, which took place that afternoon. The woman who showed up, Suzanne, was older than their eldest Pauline, perhaps thirty or thirty-five. She explained that, after eight years working in finance, she wanted to write and teach poetry for a living.

"What kind of poetry?" Wim asked.

"Confessional poetry, mostly."

"Confessional?"

"Like Sylvia Plath."

"Do you plan on sticking your head in our oven too?" Wim said.

Cindy put the kibosh on the interviews after the woman was gone, who was flustered but smiled as Cindy told her they'd be in touch soon. Wim groused, but when Cindy took the stack of emails from the desk he didn't argue.

"I'll pick six finalists," she told him. "You can veto two of them."

Cindy included both Jeremy and Suzanne in her list of six, and, miraculously, Wim didn't reject them. In fact, at dinner that night, he slid all six emails her way.

"I can't decide," he said.

"You mean now you're having trouble being discerning? What about the drug dealers and prostitutes I've surely chosen?"

Wim smiled and sipped from his glass of water. "Har har. Just choose whichever four you want."

"But I don't know how to."

"Well, how did you pick those six in the first place?"

Cindy had done exactly what she'd planned on in the first place: she looked at the time stamps of the emails and selected the first six. How else, she thought, could she make a decision? All of the messages were essentially the same: graduate students, each at one phase or another in their program, and their assistantships, fellowships, and any jobs they had on the side barely covered their living expenses. Each applicant used the same self-descriptions: studious, quiet, a team player, respectful, early-to-bed, early-to-rise. She'd been ill-equipped to make any cuts or slashes or decisions. Plus, the spread was perfect for her goal: Jeremy was a fiction writer, Suzanne a poet; the four top inquiries included a novelist, two students who wrote nonfiction, and one Old English scholar. The creative writers, Cindy noted, had been much quicker to the punch than the students in literary studies. She wasn't sure what that said about either group.

"I've been thinking," she said. "The toy room is big. We could offer two more spots if we could convince two of them to share a room."

"They're not children, Cindy. None of them are going to want to do that."

"There's no harm in trying, is there?"

Wim leaned back and raised his hands in defeat. "Alright. You do what you want. But I still want this to be my house."

"Six. That's it. I promise."

All six accepted the offer, and two of them—another poet named Patrick and an essayist named Brady who, over the summer, had a piece about his police officer father published in *Guernica*—agreed to share the toy room, having been splitting the rent on a house in Freetown whose bedrooms were connected by a hallway that wrapped behind the house's one bathroom, so they had essentially foregone any privacy for the last year anyway. All six of the new tenants moved in on the same early-August Saturday, the humidity like dog's breath and sticky as a sugared tongue. Cindy forced Wim to help, both of them dragging boxes inside while a beehive's worth of graduate students hauled in flimsy mattresses and secondhand bookshelves and writing desks. Cindy had cleaned every room, plying Windex on all of the windows and scouring the vents, vacuuming each carpet twice. She scrubbed the bathrooms until any streaks of mildew and soap scum were but a memory.

Cindy had never seen so many boxes of books, which the graduate students carried in like trophies, as if brandishing piles of Geoffrey Chaucer and Octavia Butler and Virginia Woolf was a thinking person's dick-wagging contest, a measure of one's intellectual value. Cindy herself had always been a reader; she'd even majored in English as an undergraduate, but she took a job as an office manager immediately after graduation instead of miring herself in coursework and seminar papers and thesis writing. Rather than stockading her own books she enjoyed the library, relishing its rows of organized, laminated paperbacks that she could peruse, borrow, and return, all for free. Still, she appreciated seeing the rickety Target brand particle board shelves the graduate students owned, how they filled up with books worn down with love, their spines creased, pages dog-eared, covers faded and torn from use.

She freed Wim from assisting the cavalcade at four so he could set up the grill and begin cooking the fatty brats and frozen burgers she'd picked up at Winn Dixie. Cindy imagined a welcoming party as if she were an RA and these were her freshman charges, handing them cups of lemonade or longnecks from the several six packs of hefeweizens and lemon shandies on offer. The graduate students and their helpers indulged her at dinnertime, filling paper plates with dollops of ketchup, scoops of mustard potato salad spiced with too much paprika, handfuls of potato chips. They sat on the spacious deck, exhausted and quiet, the strongest sounds the slurping of beers and squeaky pops as bratwursts exploded against teeth. They were all clustered around her frosted glass patio table, sitting on the floral-patterned upholstered chairs and a handful of folding chairs Wim had found in the basement.

"We made the right choice, don't you think?" she said, standing next to him while he poured water into the grill's slats and shivved away at the caked-on gristle.

Wim grunted and nodded.

The graduate students traipsed off to their bedrooms right after the barbecue, citing the need to set up their internet connections and start writing syllabi for their classes, but Cindy felt their presence all evening, listening from the living room for doors opening when one would shuffle to the bathroom, the pipes creaking as water rushed from the second floor down through to the basement like a tiny, muffled waterslide. Wim, of course, fell to snoring as quickly as ever that night, rolling onto his side and bunching his head under a folded pillow while Cindy tried to exhaust herself by reading Proust, who she had told herself she'd marshal through before Christmas. She was nearly finished with *Swann's Way*, though it had taken her all summer to slog through the narrator's encounter with Madame Verdurin; he was now dreaming of visiting Venice. She had nodded off regularly during her readings, and hoped Proust would provide the same narcotic effect that night. Eventually, when she'd only pushed through a single page in ten minutes and wasn't quite sure what she had read, Cindy shut the book and turned off her reading lamp and stared at the ceiling.

The house was filled with a new energy that hadn't been there since Pauline moved out nine years ago. Even though she had been the first to fly the coop while the other three stayed for almost a decade, the house had been thrown off-kilter by her absence because Pauline's room had lost its buzzy energy, the bed no longer mussed every morning, the squeaky bureau's drawers no longer thrown open so blouses and skinny jeans spilled out, the thrum of the pop songs she listened to while finishing her homework silenced.

She must have drifted off eventually, because Cindy was startled awake by the sound of the hall toilet flushing just after six in the morning. She was not bathed in a mucky swamp of her own sweat for what felt like the first time in ages; if she'd had another dream, she didn't remember it. This, to her, was the first sign that she was truly doing the right thing by filling her house with these students. Following the gurgle of the toilet came the sound of feet pounding down the stairs and eventually the smell of coffee percolating in the kitchen (she had been clear to all of the graduate students that they had full run of the appliances, that the use of the dishwasher and the laundry were all part of the deal). Cindy threw off her blankets. Wim, still an unconscious log of body heat and morning breath, snored on. She tossed on the plum terrycloth robe she kept hung on the bathroom door and padded downstairs and found Jeremy, his hair fanned out above his ears like the flappy skin of a frilled lizard. He wore a tank top that showed off lean but muscled shoulders and arms. He wasn't wearing his glasses, which made his eyes seems smaller, and he sipped from a coffee mug: *My mother isn't great, she's grand!*, a cartoonish piano, the keys askew like buckteeth, wrapped around the porcelain. Cindy recognized it as a gift that Ben, the second youngest, had given her for Mother's Day when he was twelve.

"Good morning," she said. "It looks like you've acclimated nicely."

He nodded.

"Did you sleep well? I always have a hard time falling asleep the first night in a new place." As soon as she said it, Cindy thought: *But when was I last in a new place?* She and Wim hadn't gone on a real vacation in years, not since they disastrously tried to take the kids to Myrtle Beach the summer before Pauline left for college; the house she had booked was way smaller than she expected and was situated across a busy four-lane road from the beach, and everyone had spent the entire trip bickering about one thing or another, and something was wrong with the oven so none of the meals she cooked came out right and Wim got sick, blaming—without saying a word—the undercooked chicken she tried to roast on the second night.

Jeremy smiled, a clipped tug of his lips. "Falling asleep was the easy part. Staying that way wasn't as simple. But it wasn't your house. I'm just a light sleeper. Comps are stressing me out."

"Comps?"

"Comprehensive exams." He held up a slim volume: a collection of W.H. Auden poems. "We have to pass four qualifying exams before we can formally start our dissertations. I made the mistake of picking Modern British Literature as one of them, even though I've never really taken coursework in that area."

"So why choose it?"

He shrugged. "My adviser thought it would be more versatile on the job market. Not as many creative writers study contemporary Brits as they do American writers. She thinks I'll stand out."

"Ah."

"But before I mire myself in political poetry," he said, rising, "I'm going to go for a quick jog."

"You're a morning runner, then."

"I don't know if I'd call myself a 'runner.' That makes me sound more athletic than I am. But I do go in the morning, because otherwise it gets so hot and humid, I feel like I'm inhaling cotton."

She offered to clean out his coffee mug, which he passed to her as he exited the kitchen, leaving his book on the island. Cindy picked the volume up and leafed through it; the pages like old newspaper and smelled of mildew, and several were crumbly, their edges torn like cauliflowered ears. The poems themselves were heavily annotated, lines highlighted in yellows and pinks. Several different handwritings crowded the margin, pencil and pen commenting on the rhythm and themes. She paused at "Lullaby," the only Auden poem she'd ever read in college, sighing at the simple romance that was crowded with excessive deep reading. She set the book down.

That afternoon she called Winnie for their weekly chat, an update of what her daughter was doing in Tuscaloosa where she had matriculated at Alabama the fall before, much to the chagrin of Wim, a long time LSU Tigers fan. Cindy had not informed any of her kids of the impending takeover of their childhood bedrooms by the graduate students, and she certainly hadn't mentioned her dreams. She knew she should have told them about the tenants, because sooner or later one of her children would surely visit. Winnie had spent the summer living in her sorority house, a massive, mansion-like structure with grand columns and gilded, twisting staircases and living quarters more reminiscent of penthouse suites than dorm rooms; her dues were absurd, but she paid them through her part-time waitressing gig at one of the nicest restaurants in town. Winnie, Cindy thought, was the best choice for telling the truth: she was the calmest and kindest, the one who had been least protective of her forgotten toys and the clothes she'd outgrown, often excited and willing to help sell the wares strung out on tables in the garage each year.

When Cindy told her, Winnie was silent for a moment.

"Are you guys okay, financially?" Winnie said. "Because I can send you money."

Cindy laughed and asked why in the world Winnie would think something like that.

"Well, why else would you be taking on renters?"

Cindy said the house felt too empty, too large, for just her and Wim. Four empty bedrooms gong and echo with a restlessness, a disuse that could drive a person crazy, especially after spending a lifetime filled with the noises of four loud, often-arguing children.

"Ok. But. So, where will I sleep for Thanksgiving?"

"Well. Um. We have plenty of space in the basement?"

"And what about my stuff?"

"What stuff?" Cindy felt a compression in her chest, like someone was folding a cardboard box against her sternum.

"You know, everything I didn't bring with me."

"Surely that didn't amount to much, did it?"

"I guess not, but I'm sure I left some things."

"Anything you left is packed up exactly where you left it." Cindy could feel the lie pooling in her cheeks like a buoy.

"Okay, I guess." Winnie paused. "Have you told Pauline, Derek, and Ben yet?"

"No, sweetheart. You're the first."

"Should I keep it a secret?"

Cindy wasn't sure what to say to this. She knew that Pauline would be flippant at best; after all, she hadn't made a trip to Louisiana in the three years since her husband opened his law firm in Seattle, citing busy schedules of their own and the impossibility of finding a good dog-sitter for their three labradoodles. Derek she could hardly pin down anyway—he'd spent six months last year backpacking through Europe, a trip that had made Cindy just about lose her mind because he'd had no itinerary and no cell phone she could call him on and she didn't hear from him for three months. When he finally did reappear, he stayed in Lafayette for only a week before taking off for the east coast, intending to find work in Charleston, South Carolina, a place, to her knowledge, he had never before been. What would he care about his room being taken over by a stranger?

"I worry about Ben," was all Cindy said.

Ben: only eleven months older than Winnie. He waffled and wavered over college before finally accepting a glimmering full ride to UT-Austin he'd received after submitting a stellar admissions essay. He'd written it in the form of a villanelle; the writer-in-residence, a poet, called to speak with him directly, which Cindy was sure didn't happen in real life. Ben, who spent two days crying when he was nine when the goldfish he won at the county fair—tossing a ping pong ball in a beautiful arc into its glass bowl—died in the middle of the night, discovered the morning belly-up and wormy-pink, its eyes bloated open like whole peppercorns. He demanded the fish be flushed gently down the toilet and its name—Bubbles—ensconced in magnetic letters on the fridge for a month. Ben, who had come home every summer and spring break and then remained at UT-Austin at the Michener Center for the MFA, sending home copies of his poems via regular mail, all addressed to his mother. He still lived there, teaching part-time in the undergraduate writing program and living with a girlfriend Cindy has never met. Like her other children, he left little of himself behind when he moved into his adulthood, but the transmission of his possessions took longer, Ben packing up small swaths of keepsakes and clothing on each trip home, like a worker ant carrying the tiniest crumbs to the anthill. The last time he was home he hauled one box, containing a short story he wrote in seventh grade, sheathed in a plastic cover with red slide binder, along with three pairs of socks and a battered blue teddy bear missing its right eye. At the door to his car he sputtered his lips, letting his shoulders droop after he slid the box in. He blinked at his mother and father and clapped his hands against his jeans and said, "I guess that's it," voice filled with sorrow as if he was never allowed to return again. He hadn't come home since.

"So I shouldn't tell him, then?" Winnie said.

Cindy sighed slipping into bed that first Sunday night. She had envisioned a tableau like in a Thanksgiving movie, the dining room table sighing under the weight of dishes and wine goblets, bodies brushing against one another, jokes being told, the graduate students gossiping about who they hoped was writing their comprehensive exams, what the scoop on the new Ethnic Lit professor was, whether the Americanist who'd taken a medical leave last semester because of a rumored opioid problem was coming back or not. Instead, she watched from the living room as the graduate students pattered in and out, searching the fridge for food like scavenging birds.

Wim was watching a late-night comedian's opening monologue, the volume low so the audience's laughter and applause sounded like distant lapping waves. His glasses were perched low on his nose. He reminded her of a portrait of Benjamin Franklin.

"Your tenants living up to your standards?" he said, muting the tv.

"They're *our* tenants," she said.

"Hmphf. Wasn't my idea. I think one of them already clogged the toilet."

"How do you think that but not know?"

"I heard the noise of the plunger earlier."

"So they unclogged it."

"I didn't say they didn't."

"Well, you implied it."

"Hmphf."

Cindy sighed again.

"What?"

She wasn't sure what. Even though the house was now full of bodies, something was missing. The graduate students went about their business, holed up in their rooms where they studied and played music and surfed the internet and maybe watched porn. She had envisioned a living room full of bodies watching *Jeopardy!* or *Wheel of Fortune* together like when Pauline, Derek, Ben, and Winnie were kids and got into pissing matches over who had yelled out the correct answer or solved the puzzle the fastest and would have won that trip to Aruba or Paris.

"Nothing, nothing," she said, and instead of picking up the Proust volume she turned out her bedside lamp so the room glowed with the deep-sea blue of the television's ambient light; as she willed herself to sleep, Cindy felt like she was floating across the ocean, its wordless breath hauling her down, down, down.

The rain started that night. Harsh, thick storms weren't unusual in southern Louisiana in August, daily thunderheads stomping in and pouring out inches of rain before disappearing within the hour, turning the leather-dry dirt and grass into swamps that hardened in the crispy salamander sun. But when a sharp crack of thunder shuddered Cindy awake in the middle of the night, she immediately knew this rain was different.

A gasping, coagulating feeling followed Cindy until she found Jeremy and Suzanne sitting at the kitchen island, staring out the wide windows above the sink. She stood silently next to them and watched the sheets of rain batter the porch, soak into the wood, pool on the dips in the furniture's cushions, pummel the palmettos Wim planted two summers ago.

When she thought *flood*, Cindy's neck tingled and her mouth tasted like pennies. She and Wim weren't religious even though her parents had dragged her to church every Sunday until she turned eighteen and went off to college. She'd kept up the pretense for a time, trying out different churches but finding them all way too fire and brimstone for her liking, and when she took her first philosophy class, with a professor who was clearly an atheist, she started to see the chinks in the armor of Catholicism and she stopped. She and Wim didn't even bother with a religious ceremony when they married (scandalous at the time and probably, he liked to joke, what caused his mother's heart attack when she was only in her late fifties).

But this was something else. Something achy. Something boneset. Something gold and strident.

"It's really coming down," Jeremy said, flapping a book—*A Portrait of the Artist as a Young Man* this time, one that Cindy actually had read before—against his thigh.

Suzanne nodded and yawned, stretching her arms above her head so her blouse revealed a bramble tattoo smashed against her arm pit and a toned midsection fried golden by the Louisiana sun. "I was going to go to the office today, but yeesh. I don't want to feel like a drowned cat the whole time."

Cindy called her boss and said she was going to use some of her PTO, just a day's worth, she hoped, but if the rain got any heavier, she might have to use more. Wim trudged off to his accounting office in spite of the deluge, his golf umbrella bending into the crispy wind like nothing more than a strip of paper being battered about.

The rain did get worse, and it did not stop—not Tuesday or Wednesday or all that week. On Saturday Wim trudged up from the basement (theirs was one of few houses in Lafayette with one, which Cindy had thought would be a perk), his shoes squeaky with water. The basement had never flooded or leaked before, despite concerns expressed by all of their friends when they first purchased the house. It had been well-sealed, their realtor noted, and the location was above the flood plain of the Vermillion River that snaked through town, perched on a hill in River Ranch where the soil surrounding the house, barring devastating flooding of the highest order, couldn't absorb enough water to cause leakage, the drainage system excellent and the elevation preventative.

The white shag carpet was waterlogged, the hooked legs of the pool table sodden, the lower reaches of the microfiber couch and matching recliners saturated with the algae smell of a fish tank. "We'll need new carpet," Wim said, shaking his head. "Or maybe epoxy would be better."

Cindy called Winnie, who reported that Alabama was being battered, too.

"It's strange," Winnie said.

Cindy agreed. "Even when the hurricanes come through it hardly lasts," she said. But she wasn't really thinking of hurricanes; she was reliving her dream, in which her basement was sheared away and she could see the water below, a silver lake bubbling up from the sewers, a flashing, sinewy muck carrying dead fish and human waste.

The next morning, Jeremy reported that one of his best friends was now homeless, his apartment complex totally flooded; he had woken to his own bedroom gone swampy, six inches of water crushing through the floor.

"Tell him he can come here," Cindy said without a second thought. "We have couches."

And so the seventh graduate student joined them. Cindy said nothing to Wim, hoping that he would somehow not notice. The roads were now too bad for him to drive into work, so he logged onto the laptop, hemming and hawing and scowling out the window in the office that looked out onto their street while he worked from home. The day the rains began Cindy had bustled out to Fresh Time and Adrian's Market and Winn Dixie, scouring their weekly mailers for deals. She had stocked up, jamming the pantry and refrigerator full of meats and breads and milk and cans. Wim had at first scoffed at her gloom and doom attitude, then finally nodded his thanks when she brought him a plate of food while he crunched his numbers and sighed at spreadsheets.

Campus was closed, so the graduate students hung around, whispering to one another and typing on their computers or reading in their rooms, periodically appearing on the ground floor to stare out at the rain. The weather would clear periodically, the deluge pausing, and the house would take on a strange silence that dinged and popped. Cindy opened the back door and stepped onto the porch that squelched with water. She took ginger steps to the edge and rested her hands on the soggy railing. It held steady as she looked out over the flooded yard, the water thick and deep as a creek. Less than an hour later the rain began again. Three times this happened, and on all three occasions

Cindy caught her breath when the drops stopped falling, wondering if her dreams had been wrong after all. But then the downpour would rev up again and a strange calm would settle into her chest, a knowledge that what she was doing was right and true.

Brady the essayist approached her one morning when she was alone in the living room and asked, his voice low, if his girlfriend might be able to stay for a while; the roof of her house in the Saint streets leaking, the electricity out. Cindy patted his hand and said of course.

She had been watching the news and received calls from Pauline and Ben. She told them she had plenty of supplies and although the streets weren't really navigable the house was fine. She opted not to mention the graduate students or the flooding in the basement, particularly not to Ben, who sounded like he was on the verge of tears. Austin was sunny, he said, as if this was something for him to feel guilty about. Pauline was a bit more dismissive of the rainy woes of the deep south, as if everyone living there was an idiot for taking up residence in what amounted to one big flood plain.

They had seen the aftermath of Hurricane Katrina, whose beating winds and deadly rains didn't hit Lafayette directly, pouring down buckets of water but doing nothing near the damage that smashed New Orleans and the Ninth Ward to bits. What Cindy and Wim and the kids did witness was the result of mass evacuation, the front of refugees whose cars were jammed with clothes and keepsakes, whatever people could pull into their back seats and trunks while the world around them went to hell. Over the six years that followed the hurricane the housing market in Lafayette went nuts, rental properties becoming so desirable that costs spiked, and even home values shot up to the point that even the most modest of neighborhoods became out of reach for the lower middle class, who found themselves competing for two-bedroom apartments that went for well over a grand per month: certainly not New York or San Francisco prices, but for a small city that had once been economically appealing for the less fortunate, the strain was harsh and wide-spread.

When Wim groused about the increased body count that night, she pointed out their luck.

"We're paying it forward," she said.

"It's not like anyone forced these kids to go to graduate school," he said.

"And no one forced us to be jerks."

"Hrmphf."

"It's becoming a disaster zone out there, Wim. We have to help whoever we can."

"We don't have to do anything. But if it helps you sleep at night, fine."

She still refused to tell him about the dreams; Wim would find them absurd, and she worried that if he knew that they were her primary motivation for bringing in the graduate students, he might try to get rid of them. He had lawyer friends, and the lease they'd strummed up was weak for both parties. No real penalties for unpaid rent, but also no provisions to protect the lessees from being booted at any time. She felt a strong enough assurance, though, that even if he did know about the dreams, he wouldn't drive the graduate students from the house; deep down, despite his rumblings and his moaning and groaning, she knew Wim was a kind man, all bark and very little bite. The kids, in fact, had always confessed wrongdoings to him instead of her, because even though he would glower and make a public bluster to frighten the others into not repeating the mistakes of the sinner, he rarely doled out any serious punishments. The first time Pauline drank alcohol—sixteen years old, at a neighbor kid's party, two grape-flavored wine coolers that she threw up the next morning, leading to her tear-streaked confession—he sat the whole cadre down and explained why that was dangerous, his voice gaining strength and volume with each sentence. But following his pomp and grandiosity he pulled her into the office, shut the French doors, and spoke to her in low, dulcet tones, grabbing her in a large bear hug, her snotty tears smearing against his shoulder. He later told Cindy that he'd told Pauline he loved her, that he wasn't mad at her for what she'd done but that she'd done it stupidly, without adult supervision, and to excess, and then gotten in the car with a friend. He told her, with a hand gently anchored on her shoulder, that if she ever drank again and needed to get home that she should just call, no questions asked, and he would leave the house no matter the hour and no matter how far. All he wanted, he told her, was for her to be safe. He called her his little girl, as all good fathers say to their daughters at some point, and told her the world would still be here the next day, and that her mother and father would keep on loving her.

"And maybe," he'd joked, "we'll turn you into a beer drinker instead, when you're older."

They'd laughed at that, and she'd gone off to finish her trig homework after accepting a pigeon peck on the cheek.

Cindy told the graduate students to spread the word: anyone displaced by the lashing rain who could make their way to the house was welcome. The doorbell rang several times over the next few days, and Cindy ushered in waterlogged students hauling their laptops wrapped in t-shirts, their most important books stacked in their arms, clothing tucked in rumpled shoulder bags. They looked like refugees, soaked through, shivering and grateful, their eyes glossed with disbelief and lack of sleep.

She called Winnie and updated her, then asked how the weather was in Tuscaloosa.

"It's starting to get wet here. I think one of the dorms flooded."

That word again, sending shocks of thrill, fear, and assurance through Cindy.

"I think something's going to happen," Cindy said. "You should come home."

Winnie sighed. "But how would I get there?"

It was true: the quickest route, over the Atchafalaya Basin Bridge, was not an option, as the rains had pushed the bayou up onto the dual bridge, and it had become impossible to drive in either direction, gators and eels and weeds taking up residence where bumpers and blinkers and tires belonged. If Winnie was to come home she'd have to go well out of her way; even the route swooping down through New Orleans was unsafe, and rumblings of a Katrina recurrence were starting to build like the wind before a tornado. Her only real option would be crossing all the way along I-20 through Jackson and over to Shreveport to I-49 and heading south through Alexandria.

"I still have to go to my classes next week, Mom."

"They haven't cancelled? Campus is closed here."

"Nope. I have psych first thing on Monday morning, as usual."

"That seems unsafe."

"I don't want to hurt my grades."

"I suppose you don't." But Cindy bit her lip, imagining her daughter being swept away by a primordial deluge, a dark, foamy green hand gathering her and her blonde sisters up. Cindy slept poorly that night, and not even the end of *Swann's Way* could put enough droop in her eyes to allow her to drift off. Cindy twisted and turned, rocking and groaning and throwing her head under her pillow so much that even Wim was woken up at three in the morning. He reached an arm over to her side of the bed and slipped his hand around her shoulder, pulling her close.

"What is it?" he said.

"Nothing."

"You rocking us around like we're on a roller coaster isn't nothing. Did you drink soda before bed again?"

"No, I didn't. I'm just worried about the kids, that's all."

"What about them?"

She flapped a hand in the air. "The rain. The floods." She recounted what Winnie had said about the dorm. *Flood* clamored like a wedding bell.

"Everything's fine. Except we may need a new foundation." He patted her on the arm and retracted himself back to his side of the bed. "Try to get some sleep."

Cindy did fall into a muddled sleep somewhere around five in the morning, her brain not quite shut off. She heard the front door fly open. Then the sound of footsteps: dozens of pairs marching around the dining room. They stomped through the kitchen and living room, scrounging in the refrigerator and pantry like savages who haven't eaten for days. She felt the lurching motion of the house detaching and swirling off its foundation and heard a bellowed alarm from Wim. The noise reached her ears with sluggish malaise.

She groaned, her wordless response trapped on her lips, mouth locked as if sealed with honey.

Two of each, she tried to tell Wim. *A pair of poets, a pair of novelists, and don't forget the Victorian scholars.* She felt herself drift down the stairs in her bathrobe like a matriarch, the zoo of graduate students waiting for her, the muddy smell of rain water filling the house as it drifted like a river cruiser down the street, the stairs rudderless and slippery beneath her. They looked up at her with their smeared glasses and unshaved beards and greasy hair and ill-fitting pajamas. Her charges, her mission.

At the bottom of the steps she paused and looked out the open door, which slammed against the front of the house like a slapping idiot. The front porch pitched, the bow of her ship, Cindy the captain.

Save them, a voice said through the pounding rain, bouncing through her head and replacing the thrum of drops. Cindy felt a swirl, a confidence, a knowledge.

She turned to face her charges and felt a jolt, a tug, a stir: the morning sun shone on her face, pushing through the curtains of rain, a sign of hope. The graduate students cheered. They howled. She inhaled: *Onward.*

Acknowledgments

My immediate and endless gratitude to Dr. Ross Tangedal, Brett Hill, Grace Dahl, and Amanda Leibham for their guidance and production of this book. In particular, I'm grateful to Ross for saying yes where several other people said no. I certainly will not forget it.

No book is written in a vacuum, and the supporting cast that has surrounded me over the years deserves so much credit for this book. To my parents and sisters; to my dearest friends, especially Kristen, Helen, Jeff, Jayme, Annie, Shannon, and Tracey; to my colleagues, particularly the momentous and incomparable Jacqueline and Karen; and to my teachers, Michael, Dominic, Priscilla, Barb, Robin, Joe, Monica, the other Joe, Marthe, and, of course, my dissertation adviser Daniel. Every one of you has a piece of this book in you whether you know it or not.

And thank you to the editors of the journals who published these stories, giving my voice a little amplification in a very loud world. The following stories appeared, some in slightly altered form, in the following publications:

"Transubstantiation" in *Big Muddy*
"Amphibians" in *Rio Grande River Review*
"The Itch" in *Westchester Review*
"Flytrap" in *Cardinal Sins*
"Back Swing" in *The Temz Review*
"Shark Boys" in *Quarter After Eight*
"Glass Children" in *The Meadow* (nominated for a 2019 Pushcart Prize)
"Terrarium" appears as a chapbook published by The Head & Hand Press
"Demon Lover" in *Peculiar Magazine*
"In Memoriam" in *Paris Lit Up*

Joe Baumann's fiction and essays have appeared in *Phantom Drift*, *Passages North*, *Emerson Review*, *Another Chicago Magazine*, and many others. He possesses a PhD in English from the University of Louisiana-Lafayette. He was a 2019 Lambda Literary Fellow in Fiction, and his debut short story collection, *Sing With Me at the Edge of Paradise*, was chosen as the inaugural winner of the Iron Horse/Texas Tech University Press First Book Award.

9 798986 144771